EXIT MR PUNCH

Mignon Warner

EXIT MR PUNCH

255810

BREESE
BOOKS
LONDON

First published in Great Britain by
Breese Books (A division of Martin Breese International)
164 Kensington Park Road, London W11 2ER, England

ISBN: 0 947 533 60 5

*All of the characters in this book
are fictitious, and any resemblance
to actual persons, living or dead,
is purely coincidental.*

*Typeset in 10½/12½pt Bembo by
Ann Buchan (Typesetters), Middlesex.
Printed and bound in Great Britain by
Itchen Printers Ltd., Southampton.*

PROLOGUE

The girl standing in the upstairs window abruptly turned aside, picked up her shoulder-bag and a headscarf from off the foot of the bed and then went quickly out of the room. She felt uneasy about being in the house on her own; had wanted to ask her mother to take the day off and drive over with her to Little Gidding to see her clairvoyant, Edwina Charles, but that would have only led to another scene, and she'd had enough of being told what she should do, and who she could and could not see, for one day.

A ripple of apprehension washed over her.

Sharda had promised her that this was the road to Karma; that to attain to her highest, her truest destiny, she must do as the Holy One said and make this pilgrimage back home to her roots; that no decision must be made about her life until the Moon entered her Sign on the Fourteenth, tomorrow. All would be well; nothing could go wrong now. Tomorrow this terrible black cloud that had descended upon her would be lifted forever. . .

She hesitated, shivered a little as, against her will, she suddenly found herself thinking of the warning that Sharda had once given her about her silver cord — the delicate thread running between her physical body and her astral body; that should it become severed through some deep emotional shock, a trauma of any kind, her life would be at an end as surely as if someone had plunged a knife deep into her heart.

Her violet-blue eyes clouded with anxiety. Tomorrow's New Moon suddenly seemed a long way off, as if it would never come, and she wished that Sharda were there to re-assure her that she hadn't strayed from his path, that all would be well, as he had promised her, if she did exactly as he said and returned home to her parents in Gidding to await this more favourable planetary grouping of the Moon in the Ascendant before making any major decisions concerning her career.

She started down the stairs, her uneasiness increasing with each slow step she took and aggravated by the guilt which gnawed relentlessly at her conscience in the back of her mind.

Sharda had warned her to beware of false prophets; that she must listen to none but the one true holy man.

Could it be that Edwina Charles was the false prophet he had warned her against?

She paused at the foot of the stairs, turned her head sharply and looked in the direction of the kitchen; listened tensely for any sound of movement, a footfall as someone crossed to the door. Her heart thumped hard in her breast. She was sure she hadn't imagined it, that faint scraping sound, like a drawer being opened and closed . . . The one in the sink unit under the window.

She felt confused, desperate; close to tears.

Was this it — the risk that Edwina Charles had foretold from the Tarot in being oblivious to the heavy black shadow, the dark clouds that were gathering threateningly over her life as a direct consequence of following the path which Sharda had charted for her up until the Moon entered her Sign?

She was momentarily panic-stricken; immobilised by indecision.

Who was right, Sharda or Edwina Charles? Should she stay; should she go . . . return immediately to London and face up to her problems there, at source, and stay as far away as possible from all past influences on her life, as Edwina Charles had advised time and again after reading the Tarot for her?

She drew in her breath, then let it out very slowly.

This was silly . . . She mustn't confuse issues like this. This was something so trivial it hardly bore thinking about, not when she compared it with all the other things that were slowly driving her out of her mind with worry. This was something she could handle herself — she was going to have to face him sooner or later and have it out with him face to face; it was no use running to Edwina Charles and expecting her to solve this problem for her, or asking Mike to look into it; no use thinking anybody but herself was going to tell the obnoxious little pest to get lost. After all, she had no real cause to think he was going to harm her: anyone could have stolen that lacy black bra of hers from off the clothes-line yesterday; it needn't necessarily have been him. So all right, everyone knew he was a little bit peculiar in the head, weird, but not in that way. He wasn't dangerous. To others, maybe; but not to her. At least she didn't think so. The worst he'd done was to hang about on the common at the bottom of the garden watching her bedroom window late the night before last, and then only that once so far as she knew. Those other times . . . Well, that was years ago.

She frowned. She mustn't dwell too much on this. It wasn't healthy: it made her think about things that she didn't want to remember, things that were best forgotten. She only had someone else's word for it that he used to follow her around everywhere she went, day and night, after she had quit singing in the church choir, and that he would hang about out there on the common spying on her late at night as she undressed for bed; that he had told people she was his, she belonged to him exclusively, and that no one else could have her.

This was an occupational hazard, anyway. She should be used to this sort of thing by now, men fantasising about her and chasing after her, making a general nuisance of themselves. It was the price she had to pay for the raunchy image she projected out there on stage. Men — some men, that is — thought she was really like that all the time. A raving nymphomaniac who would jump into bed with just anybody at the drop of a hat! And maybe in some strange, twisted way he felt she owed him something for her success. Her parents certainly did. To hear them talk now, they were the ones who had recognised her talent, pushed her into making a career for herself as a pop-rock singer — sacrificed everything to give her a chance to make it to the top — and yet of everyone, they'd had the least to do with her struggle to get to where she was; hadn't wanted to know; hadn't even liked her singing in the church choir when she was a kid because it meant one of them having to leave their precious television set at night to go out and fetch her home after choir practice.

People were funny about these things. She hadn't noticed it so much before, but this last trip home had been a real eye-opener. She couldn't so much as walk down the street to pick up a newspaper without, in most instances, some complete stranger approaching her like an old friend and then regaling her with some totally boring anecdote allegedly linking them intimately in the past. People acted as if they owned her; as if she owed them some special debt of gratitude for their having liked her records and having gone out and bought them. It was getting so bad that some days it was all she could do to stop herself from screaming at these people to shut up and go away and leave her be. It was Joujou they wanted to talk to, to be near, to touch, to fantasise about, not Judith Caldicott; and Joujou was in London, where Judith Caldicott had left her. Joujou, with her wild, silver mane of hair, and pink, pouting lips — her black leather mini-skirted outfits bursting suggestively open down the front of the bodice — had no place in stuffy old Gidding.

They didn't seem to understand: she simply couldn't get through to them. Joujou was a fiction; didn't really exist other than in their poor, pathetic, sex-starved imaginations!

She moved from the stairs towards the kitchen, paused on the threshold with her hand on the door which was slightly ajar; pushed it gently open.

'Hello,' she said. 'Is someone there?'

The door giving onto the untidy, rubbish-littered back garden was wide open. It was not impossible that her mother had gone off to work this morning and had forgotten to lock it behind her, but she doubted it, especially as she was still in bed and sleeping when her mother had left.

She stood in the kitchen doorway looking across the room at it. A thought suddenly occurred to her and her cheeks flushed a bright, angry pink.

'*Ben*? Is that you? Dammit, I know you're there! I meant what I said: we had some great times, but it's over, *finished*! I want you out of my life! You're driving me crazy. . .'

CHAPTER ONE

Edwina Charles put down the telephone receiver, then reached across her desk for her diary, which lay open at that day's date, and cancelled out her three o'clock appointment. She was surprised that Mr Caldicott had phoned and not Judith herself, though he hadn't specified the exact nature of his daughter's sudden illness, so it could well be a recurrence of the throat infection which had been troubling her almost constantly throughout these past few months, and that would almost certainly mean she had been given strict instructions by her doctor not to talk and to rest her voice completely. There had been an abnormal huskiness to her father's voice which had suggested that he too might be suffering from a similar kind of infection, the early autumn flu virus, perhaps, that had swept through Gidding during the past two weeks.

The cancellation nevertheless bothered Mrs Charles. There was no reason for Mr Caldicott to lie about his daughter, and yet the clairvoyant couldn't rid herself of the feeling that he had not been speaking entirely truthfully to her. If Judith herself had decided not to keep her appointment that afternoon (and somebody hadn't made this decision for her, which was the sort of thing that was apparently happening to her lately with increasing frequency), then it would have to be some matter of life and death importance to her, like her recurring throat problem, that was keeping her away and at home. Judith was still a long way off from sorting out her emotional troubles; if anything, becoming increasingly dependent on her — and on the Indian holy man, Sharda, whom she regularly consulted when in London — for guidance and reassurance; worryingly so.

Mrs Charles gazed pensively at the telephone. The Caldicotts — Judith's parents — didn't approve of their daughter's close friendship with her; but this had nothing to do with her being a clairvoyant, nor with the fact that she was thrice-divorced and had, in the opinion of some, a decidedly shady past that was directly linked with the years during which she had earned her living as a seaside, end-of-pier fortune-teller. Neither did Mrs Charles have any reason to suppose that they had voiced any strong objections to Judith's decision to consult her regularly each Wednesday afternoon for a reading of the Tarot since returning home to Gidding a month ago, partly on the insistence of her doctor, for a complete rest. It was her (Mrs Charles's) eccentric younger brother, Cyril, they disapproved of. The Caldicotts had never liked him. They would deny it, of course, but it was Cyril's interest in Judith that had prompted them to take her away from the church choir when she was a little girl.

Mrs Charles sighed a little, then reached for the telephone and dialled the number of St Stephen's vicarage. It was a lovely day, too nice to be wasted indoors. . .

The vicar's wife, Anne Blackmore, was delighted that Mrs Charles was free to resume their once-weekly get-togethers over afternoon tea at the vicarage. It was an unusually warm afternoon for September, rather stuffy and oppressive indoors, and so they sat drinking their tea on the weed-ridden terrace that Anne was always threatening to tidy up but never actually got round to doing anything about. 'Joujou . . . I mean, Judith,' she laughed as she poured tea for her guest, 'has finally deserted us again for the bright lights and mounting fame and glory of London, has she? Frank will be devastated. He's been working up the courage for days to speak to you and see if you wouldn't mind asking her to sing a special anthem at our Harvest Thanksgiving.'

Mrs Charles smiled. 'I shouldn't have thought Mr Blackmore was a pop fan.'

'He isn't.' Anne smiled mischievously. 'Just between you and me, I'm sure it's that black leather Judith almost wears that turns him on. He never misses watching her when she's got a hit in the top ten and she's appearing on television. Mind you, she's got a beautiful voice. Besides, the body gorgeous, that is. . .' Anne grinned. 'She's been having a lot of trouble with it, hasn't she? Her voice, I mean.'

'Yes . . . Her throat, actually. Some kind of viral infection that's proving stubbornly resistant to the antibiotics she's been taking for it. Though I don't know that this is why she couldn't keep her appointment with me this afternoon. Her father didn't actually say what's wrong with her.'

'I keep reading about this throat infection, and yet the impression I get is that no one really knows what the trouble is. I read somewhere the other day that it could be something quite serious: nodules, or something of that nature, growing on her vocal chords, and that maybe she'll never sing again . . . That's if they have to operate.'

Anne looked at Mrs Charles hopefully. Judith Caldicott was the local girl made good whose every 'sexploit', thought and whim, for the moment, rated equal Press and television coverage with events which one would have supposed would be of far greater National interest, and Anne was no different from anybody else: she too had been skilfully manipulated by the mass media to the point where she was consumed with curiosity about the young pop star's dramatic walk-out on an important recording session a month ago, and her sudden reappearance in her home town after having sworn publicly that she would never be seen dead there.

The vicar's wife was an attractive, fashionably-dressed, early middle-aged woman with an air of glamorous sophistication about her that was at odds, not only with her role in the local community, but with the man she had married, whom many suspected assembled his own personal wardrobe from rejects cast out from the sacks of second-hand clothing collected for the poor and needy of the parish, as suitable only for burning. There were those, of course — notably, Miss Margaret Sayer, who sat on the church council, and who was known for her antipathy for the vicar's wife — who never missed an opportunity to voice the opinion that having a fashion-plate like Anne for a wife, qualified Frank Blackmore as being one of the poorer and needier of the parish (particularly since neither of them, so far as anyone knew, had any sort of private income to supplement his traditionally modest country parson's stipend), and one could therefore hardly expect him to look any better than he did. Somebody over there at the vicarage had to make do!

Mrs Charles said, 'Hopefully, this period of rest that Judith has been having at home with her parents will take care of the problem.'

'Is that a note of doubt I hear in your voice?' Anne hesitated; smiled fleetingly at her guest. 'Judith hasn't been driving out to the village once a week to see you in search of a cure for a bad sore throat, has she?'

'I've known Judith since she was a little girl —'

Anne was eyeing her curiously; didn't wait for her to finish. 'Your brother discovered her, didn't he? While he was choirmaster at St Anthony's in Gidding?'

Mrs Charles smiled wryly. 'Her parents might argue with you on that point. And not only Mr and Mrs Caldicott, quite a number of people who have since come into her life.'

Anne gave her a knowing look. 'What about Judith? Where does she lay the credit for Joujou?'

'Ah, now that's a different matter.' Mrs Charles smiled at her. 'Ben Shipwell, the lead guitarist in her backing group, *Toy*, discovered Joujou, created that image for her.'

'Yes, I've read about him. They live together in her Gothic mansion somewhere in deepest, darkest London, don't they —? As is the fashion with young people today,' Anne added with a faint shrug.

'I believe so.'

Anne gave Mrs Charles a sly look. 'He must be missing her. . .'

Mrs Charles smiled non-committally. 'I dare say.'

Anne looked at her for a moment. She sensed that Mrs Charles had said as much as she was going to about the young pop star, and that if she wanted to learn more about her, she would have to try a far less direct approach, rethink her strategy.

'Shall I tell you what I think?' said Anne at length. 'Judith isn't going back . . . To any of it. To him, her guitarist boy-friend, or to her career. I think this throat trouble's her excuse. Her way out. I've had my suspicions all along that there was more to it. She can't cope with the life, can she —? The fame, this sex-goddess image she's built up for herself, the pressure of being on the road with her group most of the year; and now, this major motion picture she's been making in America, or they say she's going to make over there. . .'

Mrs Charles shook her head a little. 'I think you're reading far too much into things.'

'We'll see,' said Anne. She nodded her head knowingly. 'Just remember who said it to you first . . . That we've seen the last anybody's ever going to see of Joujou and *Toy*. Judith reminds me of one of those fast shooting stars one sometimes sees at night; brilliant for the short time that it lasts, but burnt out and dead and gone forever before it's hardly begun.'

Mrs Charles looked at her sharply, then turned her head and gazed out over the sadly neglected vicarage garden and into the distance at the clouds that were gathering ominously over the township of Gidding twenty-five miles to the south.

She thought of Judith, of the prophecy of the Tarot. Two picture cards from the Major Arcana of the Tarot had persistently dominated the young singer's regular Wednesday afternoon readings with her. The first *The Moon*, the second *The Fool*, a particularly bad combination of cards and difficult to interpret, the more so in Judith's case because her disillusionment and disenchantment with both her career and her lifestyle — which *The Moon* revealed only too clearly — had obsessed her to the point where the precise nature of the covert threat which this card always carries with it to be alert to hidden dangers, was eclipsed and in shadow. *The Fool* warned against hesitation and indecisiveness, that the decision Judith sought help with should be made without delay. With each reading, the eclipse of *The Moon* card became more complete, and as the ebb and flow of the tides are governed by the moon in the heavens above, so it was with Judith's life. It was ebbing away from her. Her life-flow was growing steadily weaker.

Anne considered Mrs Charles thoughtfully for a few moments, then frowned. 'I'm sorry, I've spoken out of turn, haven't I?'

Mrs Charles made no reply, but shuddered involuntarily. Her blue eyes darkened perceptibly. There had been an unexpected, totally inexplicable shift: the gradual eclipse of *The Moon* card which, in her mind's eye, she could see threatening the life of Judith Caldicott, suddenly receded, disappeared completely, only to return seconds later, and with all the shattering impact of a whirlwind, to cast a heavy black shadow over the clairvoyant herself.

'I can't think what came over me: I never should have said those things to Mrs Charles. I could've bitten off my tongue afterwards,' said Anne to her husband when confiding in him later about her *faux pas* over Judith Caldicott. Anne frowned at her husband. 'Are you listening to me, Frank? You've been miles away ever since you got back from town. . .' Her eyes widened a little. 'Don't tell me the Bishop has told you we're on the move again! It's Margaret Sayer, isn't it? You know she's got his ear; and everybody knows she can't stand the sight of me.'

'No, of course not; and it's absolute nonsense to say that Miss Sayer has Selwyn's ear,' Frank Blackmore grumbled. 'I don't know where you get these funny ideas of yours! For goodness' sake, don't go talking like that to anyone else. Selwyn told me he's more than happy with the work we've been doing here.'

'Well, then; what is it? You've got something on your mind?'

'That graffiti on Roper's wall — the one he and the Gidding Town Council are in dispute over. I drove back through the village and I noticed that Mrs Langston and Mrs Short have been out and about again with their scrubbing-brushes and buckets of paint thinners, or whatever, and they've cleaned it all up. Roper isn't going to be best pleased when he finds out: I rather think that graffiti was his *pièce de résistance*.'

Anne gave him a surprised look. 'He deliberately painted all those crude words on the wall himself? That was a bit sneaky, wasn't it?'

'Good heavens, no: I simply meant that Roper saw the graffiti as a very useful lever to get the Council to admit to their liability over the wall and do something about cleaning it up — and, while they were about it, finally repairing it before it tumbles down on top of somebody's head as they are walking past and does them a serious mischief!'

'One of Roper's prize Friesian cows, you mean,' said Anne with a wry smile. 'Hardly anybody else walks within a mile of that wall.'

'Maybe so. But it's still a pity that the Mesdames Langston and Short had to go and stir things up. There are plenty of other places they could've got to work on with their scrubbing-brushes: Roper's wall could've been left for a while longer until he and the Town Council had signed a truce. It's so senseless everybody getting all het up and nasty and spiteful towards one another about these trivial little things; and you must admit that it's been rather peaceful just lately.'

'Or in other words,' said Anne with another smile, 'since our fire-breathing village dragon, Margaret Sayer, slipped and fell and broke her thigh and has been confined to her lair. Was she sitting in her window when you drove past?'

'She was there earlier this afternoon as I was on my way over to the motorway, no doubt watching me through her binoculars as is her wont; but as I've said, I came back the long way through the village. I didn't want the rain chasing me all the way home from Gidding. You know I hate driving on the motorway at the best of times, let alone when it's bucketing down.' He frowned; gazed absent-mindedly at the framed set of three, atmosphere-stained, Victorian cricketing prints that were hanging crookedly on the wall near the french door of his embarrassingly patched and threadbare-looking study. 'I really must do something about getting Jack Graves to fix those windscreen-wipers before winter sets in.'

He was quiet for a moment: then, abruptly, he turned his head from the prints and smiled at his wife. 'So,' he said, 'you've put your foot in it with our illustrious clairvoyant and made her cross, have you?'

Anne looked pensive. 'Mrs Charles's reaction to my apology for having spoken out of turn about Judith Caldicott was really quite peculiar. I've felt upset about it ever since she left. I got the distinct impression that in saying the things I did, I made her see something.' She paused reflectively. 'I'm not quite sure exactly what I mean, but what I think I'm really trying to say is that Mrs Charles was suddenly given a quick glimpse into the future — Judith's future, that is — and she realised that there was something terrible waiting for the poor girl there. Or maybe —' Anne suddenly looked very frightened '— maybe it wasn't Judith at all: maybe it was somebody else, somebody much closer to home. Herself, perhaps. Or me,' she put in with a shiver. Her eyes widened anxiously. 'That's silly, isn't it, Frank?'

'Very silly,' he assured her. 'The future belongs to God. Only He knows what lies ahead.'

'Yes, but —'

'No buts about it, my dear. Now, let's have some tea, shall we? Oh, I don't suppose you thought to mention the Harvest Thanksgiving Service to Mrs Charles while she was here? It would be wonderful, a real *coup de grâce*, if she could get young Judith to come along and sing specially for us.'

Yes, thought Anne. *Wonderful, but not very likely ever to happen. Not if that look she'd seen on Mrs Charles's face shortly before she left this afternoon was to be taken as a portent of things to come. Something terrible was going to happen. . .*

CHAPTER TWO

The rain and the strong winds driving it reached Little Gidding shortly before seven o'clock that evening, and with a suddenness and such force that Mrs Charles was obliged, as was everyone else living in the small village, to hurry from room to room securing all windows against it. She was fastening the catch on the last of the casement windows in her sitting-room when the telephone rang.

It was Ruth Caldicott, Judith's mother. She had a hard, common voice, and she sounded annoyed; wasted no time in explaining her reason for contacting the clairvoyant. 'Judith's father and I don't like the idea of her driving home at this hour of night in all this wind and rain. She hasn't had her licence for very long, as you probably know, and we wondered . . . well, has she left your place yet?'

Mrs Charles hesitated momentarily before replying; frowned. 'I'm afraid I haven't seen Judith at all today, Mrs Caldicott. She cancelled her appointment with me. I understood from Mr Caldicott, who phoned on her behalf, that she was unwell and that she'd be staying at home in bed today.'

There was a pause, then Mrs Caldicott wrapped her hand carelessly over the mouthpiece and Mrs Charles heard her, very faintly, speaking animatedly to someone with her, presumably Mr Caldicott. A moment later, his voice came down the line, minus the pronounced huskiness that Mrs Charles recalled from her previous telephone conversation with him that day, though he was speaking very loudly and sounded as if he were in an extremely bad temper, which would undoubtedly account for some variation in his tone of voice.

'Caldicott here!' he barked at her. 'Now, what's all this rubbish about a phone call from me?'

Mrs Charles hesitated again; frowned to herself. Then she said, 'Good evening, Mr Caldicott . . . As I was telling your wife a few moments ago, a man identifying himself as being you, Judith's father, phoned me shortly before lunch today and told me that Judith was unwell and that she wouldn't be able to keep her three o'clock appointment with me today.'

'And you believed him?' he snarled. 'You know who Judith is, what she is, the kind of sex maniacs that are around everywhere today . . . You mean to say you didn't phone back and check?' Mr Caldicott lowered the receiver a few inches from his face and spoke to his wife. 'I don't believe this . . . How could anyone be so stupid?' He spoke back into the mouthpiece again. His voice quivered with rage. 'What kind of an idiot are you anyway?'

'I appreciate your dismay, Mr Caldicott,' said Mrs Charles, 'but I had no reason to doubt that this man was other than who he said he was.'

'Well, I didn't phone you, and Judith certainly isn't here, in her room, in her bed, or anywhere else in the house!'

'No,' said Mrs Charles, 'and I'm afraid she's not here, either, Mr Caldicott. I think that in the circumstances, you shouldn't waste another moment . . . I would advise you to contact the police immediately and notify them of her disappearance.'

'Don't you worry, I intend to! You haven't heard the last of this, Madam whoever you bloody-well call yourself, I promise you that!'

Mrs Charles pulled her head back sharply from the receiver as Mr Caldicott slammed down the telephone. She drew in her breath and closed her eyes for a moment, then quietly replaced the receiver in its cradle. Then she sat down to wait.

It took longer than she expected for the police to call on her, and while she had known, bearing in mind that one of Judith's uncles was a policeman, and from her father's attitude towards her when they had spoken on the telephone earlier that night, that Mr Caldicott was going to create a considerable amount of fuss about Judith's alleged disappearance, she was taken completely by surprise, and then dismayed when, at a few minutes to midnight, she opened her front door to find Detective Chief Superintendent Clive Merton of the Gidding Constabulary waiting without to speak to her about the missing girl. She had known the Chief Superintendent long enough to need no explanation for his involvement in the search for Judith Caldicott. This was not going to be an inquiry into the present whereabouts of a missing, emotionally-disturbed pop star. This was now either an abduction, or worse, a murder investigation.

Merton acknowledged Mrs Charles's greeting with a brief nod of his head and, at her invitation, stepped inside immediately out of the steadily rising wind and rain. He was a big, aggressive-looking man with a blunt, forthright manner, and with no liking for what he called '*the lunatic fringe*', which included fortune-tellers and in particular, the strikingly attractive, middle-aged clairvoyant facing him now who had twice got the better of him on local murder investigations. He was never entirely at ease in her presence, never knew quite how to address her, and after a slight hesitation, invariably settled for *Madame*, the title she had used as a seaside fortune-teller and which she occasionally still used professionally in conjunction with her real name, Adele Herrmann. 'Edwina' Charles was the feminine of her last husband's forename, and rather more suited, she had felt, to her semi-retirement to a sleepy little village in the heart of rural England.

Mrs Charles noted Merton's reluctance to look her directly in the eye, and it was with a growing sense of foreboding that she waited for him to speak.

'I very much regret having to make this visit to you, Madame; especially at this late hour of the night. We've had our differences in the past, we've often not seen eye to eye over things, but I confess that coming out here to see you tonight hasn't been easy for me. I only wish it could be otherwise; but I felt that in the circumstances, you'd prefer to hear this from me personally . . .' Merton paused; sighed heavily. 'I deeply regret having to inform you, Madame, that your brother, Cyril Forbes, is at the present moment in police custody and being driven to the Gidding Constabulary where he will be questioned further in connection with our inquiries into the murder of Judith Caldicott, also known as Joujou.'

It was a few moments before Mrs Charles spoke. Then she nodded her head and said, 'Thank you for your courtesy in coming here specially yourself to tell me this, Chief Superintendent. It was kind of you, and I appreciate it.' She turned from him and went into her sitting-room and sat down.

He followed her after a moment; paused hesitantly in the doorway looking at her. 'For what it's worth, Madame . . . I'm truly sorry about this.'

'Yes, I'm sure you are,' she said. 'Thank you.'

'Will you be all right?' He frowned slightly. 'Is there someone you'd like to come and be with you tonight?'

She shook her head. 'No, I'll be all right, thank you.'

He nodded. 'I'm sorry about this, but you do appreciate that there'll be a number of questions I'll need to ask you about your relationship with the dead girl; though in the circumstances, the morning will be soon enough.'

'Yes, of course. . .' Mrs Charles hesitated. 'My brother — When may I see him?'

'I'll let you know.'

'Has he told you anything?'

Merton shook his head. 'We haven't been able to get anything out of him yet. He appears dazed. . .'

Mrs Charles nodded her head. 'It's Wednesday, Mr Merton. That's why Cyril won't speak to you. Tomorrow he'll be his normal self again and he'll tell you everything you want to know.'

'I'm afraid that with the weight of evidence we have against him, that's going to be a mere formality. There isn't the slightest doubt in my mind that he killed the girl.'

She looked at him steadily. 'And there isn't the slightest doubt in my mind, Chief Superintendent, that my brother is completely innocent!'

David Sayer looked at the clairvoyant sympathetically. 'I'm sorry, Madame, but you've simply got to face facts. The girl put up one hell of a struggle; clawed your brother all down one side of his face.'

Mrs Charles looked pale and strained, as if she hadn't slept at all during the night. She got up from off the sofa and went and stood by the window looking out over her storm-battered front garden.

David, an ex-Detective Chief Superintendent of Police and a personal friend of both Mrs Charles and Clive Merton, watched her thoughtfully for a moment. Like Merton, David was inclined to feel hesitant about addressing her informally, despite their growing friendship and successful collaboration on a number of difficult murder investigations, and felt more comfortable with her professional title. For her part, she used (he presumed for the same reason) his former police rank, Superintendent, in preference to calling him by name when in conversation with him.

Finally, he asked, 'How much has Merton told you?'

'Very little; and I deliberately didn't press him for any details so as to avoid embarrassing him should he have had to refuse to tell me what I wanted to know,' she replied.

'Knowing Clive, he'll have appreciated that gesture from you,' he said with a nod. 'It's an awkward situation for him, and it's probably why he's been so forthcoming with me about everything: he knows I'll give you whatever assistance you need to see you through this unpleasant episode over your brother.' He hesitated. Then he went on, 'Your brother and I had our ups and downs while I was stationed over there at Gidding, but I can't honestly say that he ever struck me as being dangerous. Eccentric, maybe; and if you'll forgive me for saying so, something of a pain in the neck. But a killer —?' He shook his head slowly. 'Merton, unfortunately, doesn't share my views.'

'Then we're just going to have to convince him how wrong he is, aren't we?'

Mrs Charles didn't look at David as she spoke. She was still gazing out of the window, her thoughts apparently miles away. He watched her in silence. It was some years ago now, before his promotion to Chief Superintendent, but he had once seriously contemplated formally charging her with murder and the theft of a valuable diamond necklace. She herself had proved him wrong on that occasion, vindicated her name completely. He doubted that she would be able to do the same for her brother. It had only ever been a matter of time before Cyril Forbes landed himself in serious trouble with the law.

Clearing his throat a little, David said, 'I take it that Merton hasn't been back to see you yet about the phone call you say you had from someone yesterday morning cancelling the girl's appointment with you?'

Mrs Charles turned her head and looked at him. There was a slight edge to her voice when she spoke. 'There *was* a phone call, Superintendent!'

'I'm sorry . . . Force of habit, I'm afraid.' The wry smile he gave her wasn't returned.

'No,' she said after a moment. 'Merton hasn't called back.' She spoke meditatively. 'It's the phone call that really concerns me. Unless I'm very much mistaken, the police will do their utmost to prove that it was Cyril who phoned in order to lure me away from here so that I wouldn't be in when Judith arrived for her three o'clock appointment — which we all now realise, of course, she'd apparently had every intention of keeping with me.'

'Would your brother have known what you'd do —? I mean, that you'd get in touch with the vicar's wife and tell her you had a free afternoon?'

'The thing I must concern myself with is what Merton's going to think Cyril expected I'd do,' she pointed out in a slow, reflective voice. 'I'm sure you'll agree with me that not just the police, everybody, will say that Cyril planned it so that when Judith arrived here and discovered that I wasn't in, she'd drive on down the road to his place to find out where I was.'

David shrugged a little; made no comment.

She sighed. 'I'm sorry, this must be very difficult for you, caught in the middle, as it were; and I want you to know that I understand perfectly how you must be feeling. For my part there'll be absolutely no hard feelings if you wish to excuse yourself from any further involvement in the matter. I'd just

like to say how grateful I am to you — and to Clive Merton —
for the kindness and courtesy you've both shown me.'

'Good Lord, Madame: you talk as if I want no part of this!
I've told you how I feel . . . I respect Merton — and quite
frankly, were I in his shoes, with the evidence he has against
your brother, I would act no differently, I'd have no alternative; but I'm not in his shoes, I'm a free agent now, thanks to
this dicky ticker of mine —' he lightly tapped his chest;
grinned crookedly '— and like you, I think he's making a
mistake. I even half suspect that there are certain aspects of the
investigation —'

He broke off; frowned. 'It's too easy, too convenient . . .
This sort of crime . . . well, one usually has to look no further
than the victim's immediate family — the girl's father, her
boy-friend. . .'

She looked at him. 'Are you saying that it was a sex crime?'

'You didn't know?' David seemed surprised. 'There was no
physical evidence to suggest that the girl had been sexually
assaulted, even though she was in a semi-undressed state and
was found with her brassiere tied round her neck. Whoever
killed her might've been disturbed by someone, or something,
and he strangled her before things got that far — to stop her
from crying out, perhaps. She was strangled with the bare
hands: then, after she was dead. . .' He paused.

Mrs Charles looked at him questioningly. 'Yes, Superintendent?'

'Whoever strangled her, afterwards severed her vocal
chords with a sharp knife. The police are still looking for the
weapon — a kitchen knife, they think.' He hesitated for a
moment, then he said, 'It was an expert job: her killer knew
exactly what he was doing . . . Which again looks bad for your
brother.'

She looked at him curiously. 'How do you make that out?'

'Apparently it's common knowledge that your brother was
very angry when the girl gave up the formal voice training
he'd organised for her and she took up pop singing instead.'

'Oh,' she said, and nodded her head.

'Well . . . Is that true?

'He was disappointed, yes; but as for being angry. . .' She paused; considered for a moment. 'No, I very much doubt it. He himself forsook a career in the opera, you may remember my telling you once, because he preferred to be a children's entertainer.'

David looked uncomfortable.

Mrs Charles spoke sharply. 'What is it, Superintendent? I'd be obliged if you'd be perfectly frank with me, regardless of how unpleasant what you may have to say to me might be.'

He shrugged. 'You know how it is with this sort of thing. The first hint of a good story, especially one involving violent crime and sex, and the newspaper reporters are hot on the trail.' He looked at her for a moment. 'I believe there was an incident some years ago between your brother and one of the little girls he'd been entertaining with some magic tricks at a children's party . . . No formal charges were laid, as I understand it —'

Mrs Charles cut in, 'Because there were no grounds for complaint. The child in question approached my brother as he was packing up his magic apparatus at the close of the afternoon's entertainment and threatened that if he didn't give her some of the sweets he'd handed out to his various helpers during the show, she'd tell her mother that he'd made an improper suggestion to her.' She looked at him sternly. 'I'm quite sure you don't need me to tell you that little girls are not always the sweet, innocent angels they seem; and this was one of the reasons why Cyril decided that, as a bachelor, it might be wise if he were, in effect, to place a barrier between himself and his audience by setting up a booth and becoming a Punch and Judy man.' She hesitated for a moment. Then she said, 'Somebody certainly hasn't wasted much time; and I must say I find myself very curious to know how the Press got hold of this story.'

'A friend of the Caldicotts' — somebody who knows P.C. Caldicott, Judith's uncle — knew the people concerned, the little girl's parents. They apparently believed her story.' David frowned a little. 'I'm afraid there's not much doubt that this is going to prove to be a very ugly case before it's all over and done with. Your brother has, unfortunately, rather laid himself wide open . . . what with his problem with Wednesdays — you know, the sinister way he lurks about out there in the fields every Wednesday waiting for — what is it he calls it . . . *'The Coming?'* — and all this talk of his about U.F.O.'s and extra-terrestrial beings picking this particular spot of the English countryside to land their spacecraft and then colonise . . . not to mention that rocketship he's supposed to be building out there in his oast-house! Even the point you've just raised about his being a bachelor isn't going to pass without comment, you know. The fact that the girl's killer chose to strangle her and then tied her brassiere round her neck could mean he's sexually impotent, incapable of having a normal sexual relationship with a woman . . . Though I'm not for one moment suggesting that this is the case with your brother and that this explains why he has elected to remain single,' he put in quickly, and with a slight frown. 'So one way or another, the Press is going to have a field day with this little lot.'

Mrs Charles looked at him thoughtfully. 'What you just said a moment ago about Wednesdays . . . While I'll admit that Cyril is still very peculiar on this particular day of the week, it's nevertheless been some months since he's wandered about in the fields of a Wednesday. Perhaps for even as long as a year. Nowadays, he always spends his Wednesdays locked up in the oast-house.'

David shook his head. 'Not yesterday he didn't. And that's by his own admission. He reckons he spent it — the afternoon, anyway — in Roper's field . . . the one out the back of the dairy. He claims he completed some computations on a special computer he's been working on in the oast-house which proved conclusively that this space landing he's been expecting was going to take place yesterday afternoon at a few minutes after three o'clock, slap bang in the middle of Roper's precious blue-ribbon Friesians! The only trouble is, nobody saw him; and if he was where he said he was when he said he was — this is at three o'clock yesterday afternoon when, according to the pathologist, the girl died — at least two people should've seen him . . . One of them, at least, an unimpeachable eye witness!

Mrs Langston of Langston and Short fame — the pair who travel round the countryside with buckets and mops cleaning up the graffiti Gidding's Town Council won't do anything about — and my Aunt Margaret, who was sitting in her living-room window all afternoon and who swears that your brother never walked along the road as and when he said he did.'

Mrs Charles stared at him. David continued, 'According to him, he cut back across the fields to his place when he realised that something must've gone wrong with his calculations, these little green men he expected to arrive from outer space weren't going to turn up; and he admits that no one from the village saw him . . . This was somewhere around five o'clock, he thinks. He's not sure.'

'By this do you mean that Cyril saw your aunt sitting in her window when he went past earlier in the afternoon and that he suggested to the police that they should ask her to corroborate his story about his whereabouts at the precise time of the crime?'

David nodded. 'And Mrs Langston. She apparently looked over Roper's stone wall (he says) and stared straight at him while he claims he was in the field. At barely five feet tall, Agnes Short was, of course, quite literally too short to see over the top of that particular wall, as you probably know.'

'How extraordinary,' Mrs Charles murmured. She hesitated for a moment, then asked, 'What did Cyril say happened next, after he'd returned home from Roper's field later in the day?'

'Well, according to him, he went straight back into the oast-house and continued working on his computer, going back over his arithmetic. He claims he didn't go inside the house until a few minutes before the police arrived soon after eight p.m. They'd spotted Judith Caldicott's flashy red sports car parked up by his house as they were on their way here to question you about the phone call you'd told the girl's people you'd had from Mr Caldicott during the morning, and they naturally went no further. The front door wasn't locked, and when your brother didn't answer the bell, they simply walked straight in and there he was, standing in his living-room looking down at the girl who was lying stretched out on a settee . . . Strangled, as I've said, and with her throat expertly cut about and her black lace brassiere tied neatly round the wound like a bandage. The boys in blue took one look at your brother, at some fresh scratch marks on his face, and . . . well, what would you think?'

'What was Cyril's explanation for the scratches?'

'He claims he got caught up in some blackberry bushes as he was crawling through a fence after he'd finished in Roper's field. He's got all the answers, but I'm afraid they simply don't add up.'

'That one does.' Mrs Charles spoke very quietly. She looked at him gravely. 'Judith didn't have any finger-nails . . . none, that is, to speak of. She was a chronic nail-biter, has bitten her nails ever since I've known her. When she appeared on stage she wore false ones. And to the best of my knowledge, that's the only time she ever wore them; when she was performing in front of a live audience, or for the television cameras.'

CHAPTER THREE

As Mrs Charles walked up to the Caldicotts' front door, she pondered over David's parting remarks to her when she had left him a few moments earlier. He was right, of course: Judith's lack of finger-nails did not prove conclusively that it was other than she who had inflicted those damning scratches on Cyril's face. Mrs Charles also had to agree with David that Clive Merton would be wasting no time in having a search made of the scene of the crime for some suitable weapon that Judith might possibly have grabbed up and desperately struck out with as her killer mercilessly tightened his stranglehold on her throat, and which might similarly account for Cyril's facial scratch marks.

Mrs Charles had asked David if she might accompany him back to Gidding and, reluctantly, he had dropped her off outside the Caldicotts' shabby, semi-detached house on the outskirts of the town. A week or two after Judith had returned to her parents' home, she had told Mrs Charles that she had signed a contract to purchase a much larger, detached house for them on a new housing development nearby, but that it would be some months before construction work on the property was completed and the house was ready for the family's occupation.

Moments after Mrs Charles and David had drawn up on the road, a young man in his mid-to-late twenties wearing a black anorak over the uniform of a police constable, had been admitted to the house. David identified him as being Judith's uncle, Michael Caldicott. The plain anorak, and the fact that he was wearing nothing on his head, indicated that he was off duty, and in the event, it was he who answered the door when Mrs Charles knocked on it a minute or two after David had driven off, on her insistence, and left her (as she had put it) to her own devices.

Photographs of both Mrs Charles and her brother Cyril had appeared in the local newspaper that morning under the boldly obtrusive (and both provocative and highly emotive) headline, *'EXIT MR PUNCH: JUDY FOUND BRUTALLY MUR-DERED!'*, and she watched the hostility come into Michael Caldicott's eyes as he recognised her.

A woman's voice from somewhere inside the house, called out shrilly — 'Who is it, Mike?' — before either of the two people standing at the door had had a chance to speak to one another, and a moment later, Ruth Caldicott appeared in the hall. She was a slovenly-looking woman of about forty, only half-dressed — she was wearing a sloppy, faded blue towelling bathrobe over a grubby, peach-coloured slip — and her platinum blonde hair was set in large, shocking-pink plastic rollers. Her face was hard and heavily made-up, which gave Mrs Charles the impression that she was either getting ready to go out somewhere special, or was about to receive guests.

'You'd have a damn cheek coming here!' she snarled when she saw the clairvoyant.

'Only if it really was my brother who killed your daughter, Mrs Caldicott, which I assure you it wasn't,' said Mrs Charles. 'I've come to offer you and Mr Caldicott my deepest condolences, and to say how dreadfully sorry and distressed I am over what has happened. I also wanted to assure you that I intend to do everything in my power to find out who made that phone call to me yesterday in your husband's name.'

Mrs Charles spoke calmly and with a firmness that for the moment completely disarmed Ruth Caldicott, who looked sullenly at her brother-in-law as if annoyed that he hadn't suggested to her that there was a possibility that someone other than Cyril Forbes had murdered her daughter.

'You can take your pretty speeches and clear off my property right now,' said her husband, Ron, coming out of the living-room and into the hall. He was an older version of his brother, Michael: tall, with rapidly thinning, dark hair and an unusually high colour; and he was very hostile . . . The kind,

Mrs Charles thought, who would have a permanent chip on his shoulder. In fact, she was even inclined to think the same thing of Michael Caldicott to whom, for some inexplicable reason, she had taken an instant dislike.

Ron Caldicott continued, 'We all know who made that phone call. That's if there really was one. It was that weirdo, Forbes — your brother.'

'No, Mr Caldicott: I was the one who spoke to this man on the phone and I assure you it wasn't him.'

'Well, you would say that, wouldn't you?' he retorted. 'His sister is going to try and do everything she can to shield him, isn't she?' His eyes blackened with fury and he brought up his right arm and angrily jabbed his forefinger at her. 'That pervert should've been locked up years ago, and you know it! Everybody knows about him . . . He's cracked in the head!'

Michael Caldicott looked at Mrs Charles and said, in a cold, hard voice, 'I think you'd better leave. You shouldn't have come here.'

Mrs Charles met his gaze steadily for a moment; then she looked at Mrs Caldicott (whose facial expression suggested that she would have liked her menfolk to take some more positive, physical action in support of their request that their unwelcome visitor should leave), and said, 'I'm sorry, truly sorry, Mrs Caldicott. . .' Then she turned and walked away.

She found David waiting for her in his car around the corner, despite her having insisted that she would make her own way home on the bus.

'I hate to say it,' he said as she climbed in beside him, then momentarily closed her eyes and sighed, 'but I told you so.'

'Yes, I know, but it was something I simply had to do. I know some would say that calling on the Caldicotts displayed a high degree of insensitivity on my part and was in appalling bad taste in the circumstances, but if I hadn't faced them at the earliest opportunity available to me, it would've been tanta-mount to my saying that I fully agreed with them that Cyril is guilty of killing their daughter.'

David made no comment. He could understand her motives, but he still thought she had been unwise to approach the Caldicotts herself, and that this was something she should have left entirely to him. He was the one to talk to the Caldicotts and see what he could learn of Judith's last hours with them.

'From the short time you were there, I guess you didn't get an opportunity to make some reference to the phone call,' he said after a moment.

She sighed again, very faintly. 'It's as I thought: everyone's convinced that it was Cyril. There was certainly no doubt in Mr Caldicott's mind that it was my brother who phoned me.'

'Could it have been him?' he asked, starting up the car; and then, before she had a chance to reply: 'These are questions we must ask ourselves and not be afraid to answer honestly if we are to arrive at the truth about what really happened yesterday.'

'Yes, I know,' she said. 'Forgive me if I appear a little churlish and am always on the defensive, but I'm sure you can understand how very distressed I'm feeling about all of this. Cyril, in my opinion, is every bit as much a victim — though, admittedly, of a much lesser crime — as poor Judith; and although I'm not normally in the least bit negative in my outlook on things, I very much fear that this is one scrape he's somehow managed to get himself into, that I'm not going to be able to get him out of. But to answer your question —' She paused and smiled fleetingly at him. 'That's in case you think I might be trying to avoid answering it . . . Honestly and truthfully, no: it definitely wasn't Cyril. The man I spoke to had a husky voice, as if he had a heavy head cold. Cyril's voice is high-pitched.'

'I don't want you to take this the wrong way, but what about these voices your brother uses for all the different characters in his 'Punch and Judy' show? He has to be something of an actor to do that sort of thing, doesn't he?' David hesitated; looked at her. 'If this thought has occurred to me, it's going to occur to others,' he pointed out. 'We've got to examine every possibility, the way everyone else will, and satisfy ourselves completely that we've covered all the angles.'

She made no reply.

'All right,' he said with a sigh. 'We're looking for a man with a husky voice. A genuine husky voice or an assumed one?'

She shot him a quick look. 'Aren't you asking me the same question about Cyril — whether or not he's an actor — but in different words?'

'Was he ever an actor?'

'He's done some pantomime at various times. Not recently, though.'

'In Gidding?'

'Yes, once.'

David grimaced. 'Then they'll find out about that . . . The Press and Merton — that's if they're looking for some means of convincing themselves that it was your brother on the end of the line. Any chance that this chap was using something to muffle his voice — speaking through a handkerchief?'

Mrs Charles considered the question. Then she said, 'No, I don't think so: it was, as I've said, a husky voice, but I had no difficulty in hearing what was being said to me. It certainly wasn't in any way a menacing voice, which is the type of thing one would normally associate with a voice that had been disguised in the way you've suggested, with a handkerchief or a cloth of some kind covering the mouthpiece. I'm not sure if I'd recognise it if I heard it again, particularly if the huskiness was deliberately created for the purpose of disguising the caller's real voice. And I am going to hear that voice again.' She nodded her head slowly. 'That's the one thing I am sure of. I know the person I spoke to yesterday — maybe not as well, though, as he knows me . . . Or has made it his business to know me. And sooner or later he and I are going to speak to one another again. My problem is going to be in recognising his voice without its husky overtones. . .' Her own voice tailed off thoughtfully.

'What are you getting at?'

'I thought about it all night, and it's this —the phone call I received — that makes everything look so black for Cyril. I'm talking, of course, about my regular visits of a Wednesday afternoon to the vicarage. . .'

'This is something that's been puzzling me —' David admitted. 'Why you put off these visits of yours to the vicarage in the first place. It wasn't as though Judith couldn't have made it some other time, surely? She wasn't working or anything like that while she was visiting her parents, was she?'

'It had to be a Wednesday, Judith insisted on it . . . Because it was half-day closing in the village; and, as you know, Little Gidding on a Wednesday afternoon is as quiet as the grave, there's hardly a soul about.' Mrs Charles paused for a moment. Then she said, 'Judith couldn't cope with it, with being a pop star and a sex symbol; the adulation, the artistic demands that were constantly being made on her by her record company and the promoters . . . people wanting to talk to her all the time and hanging onto every word she said; her fans wanting to touch her and be near her. It had all got on top of her to the point where she was well on her way, in my opinion, to a complete physical and mental breakdown. She wanted to get out of the business altogether, and she came to me in the hope that I'd reassure her over certain advice she'd been given by her guru — an Indian holy man she'd been consulting in London — and that I'd help her to make the break.'

'By telling her the future would still look rosy for her if she took the plunge and threw in the towel, and that she wouldn't regret it?'

'Judith had to be given time, a little breathing space first, a chance to escape the spectre of Joujou which she felt had got out of control and was threatening to take her over so completely that she — Judith Caldicott, the real person — ceased to exist any more. We were a long way off from examining what the future could hold in store for her. For Judith Caldicott, the person she really wanted to be. The present was proving difficult enough for her to cope with, let alone expecting her to tackle the future . . . A future without Joujou and her backing group *Toy*, that is.'

'Which she didn't have anyway,' he pointed out.

'No, as it happens,' agreed Mrs Charles.

'What about this guru of hers? What was his panacea for all that ailed her?'

'It was on his advice that she walked out of that important recording session of hers down in London a few weeks ago and returned home to Gidding; although her doctor also felt it was sensible, in the circumstances —'

'How did you see it?' he asked when she paused. 'In the circumstances,' he added.

She shook her head a little. 'It was a terrible mistake —'

'Is that with hindsight?' he asked with a wry smile. 'Or is this something you actually told the girl to her face?'

'Broadly speaking, I advised her that she was only delaying the inevitable; that she should return to London and the sooner the better. Coming home — or, in other words, misguidedly trying (as I believe she was) to recapture some aspect of the past — merely compounded her problems, gave them an added dimension which in some way eclipsed her entire future. I tried but failed, failed to convince her that I could help her . . . If, that is, she heeded my advice and returned to London and her life there as quickly as possible.'

'Between the two of you — you and the guru — the poor girl mustn't have known whether she was coming or going,' David commented in a dry voice.

'No, quite,' agreed Mrs Charles. She did not take offence at his remark. She valued his friendship far too much to allow his scepticism of clairvoyance, which he had never made any attempt to conceal from her, to damage their special relationship in any way.

'What went wrong?' he asked after a moment. Then, in response to her questioning look: 'You said you tried but failed . . . Why?'

Mrs Charles shrugged faintly. 'After my initial warning, Judith refused to let me help her. She still clung to her weekly visits to see me for a reading of the Tarot, but without her full co-operation, I could do no more than sit and watch helplessly as the shadow hanging over her grew darker.'

'A kind of suicide?' he suggested.

'Only if she herself knew the reason for the shadow. Perhaps she did; I'm not sure. Judith was very much a *now* person, completely immersed in the present. Anything that she might've said or done to somebody, or that had been said or done to her, no longer concerned her. This suggests to me that the shadow probably had its origins deeply rooted in yesterday, in something terrible that happened way back in the past. I am inclined to think that Judith hadn't entirely forgotten this unpleasant episode of her life, she simply didn't attach any great importance to it any more, as was her nature. One of the cards from the Tarot which repeatedly dominated her readings was *The Moon*. It's a dangerous card in that it has the power, like the silvery light of the moon above, to bewitch and blind the seeker — in this instance, Judith — to some terrible danger that is lurking constantly in the background awaiting the appropriate moment to rear up and strike out. Always, I might add, with devastating consequences.'

They drove in silence for a while. Then Mrs Charles looked at David thoughtfully and said, 'Of course . . . I should've seen this before. Everything points to it . . . Ron Caldicott is absolutely right. Someone *is* shielding Judith's killer. Someone, almost certainly a woman, knows who killed her, and she's protecting him.'

David stared at her. She nodded her head. 'Yes, definitely.' She spoke softly; gazed reflectively into space. *The Moon* card represents the feminine in us all; in Judith, in her killer . . . a man with abnormally strong feminine influences. Yes, a woman, Superintendent. Judith's killer is dominated by a very determined, very dangerous woman.'

CHAPTER FOUR

Mrs Charles walked slowly along the road towards the village. The day was grey and chilly, not at all pleasant after the prolonged Indian summer they had been enjoying, and which had finally been brought to an abrupt end by last night's rainstorm. David had left her shortly before lunch with the promise that he would get back to her as soon as he could with anything he could dig up on the Caldicotts for her. He was surprised at her request for information on the murdered girl's family, but, as she had pointed out, she had to start somewhere and they were her only real lead. The Caldicotts' hostility was natural and normal enough, but little else about them fitted her expectations; and she was particularly curious to know more about a mother who, after having been told less than twenty-four hours earlier that her only child was dead, brutally murdered, could even think of putting her hair up in rollers, let alone bother with making up her face.

Merton still hadn't been back to see her about her mysterious husky-voiced telephone caller, and at length (and bearing in mind that Merton more than likely considered that he knew the identity of the man on the other end of the line, anyway), she had decided not to wait in, she was wasting valuable time. David had expressed the view that they had approximately forty-eight hours in which to discover who had killed Judith; that at the end of this period of time, which was as long as the police were legally permitted to hold Cyril without making any formal charges, Merton would in all probability make an application to the Gidding Magistrates' Court for Cyril to be remanded in custody for seven days pending further police inquiries.

The long road leading from the motorway into the village was deserted, much as Mrs Charles imagined it would have been at the same time the previous afternoon when her brother was allegedly walking along it in the same direction as she was now towards Roper's dairy. David had made no pretence of the fact that it was this part of the statement that Cyril had made to the police concerning his activities during the previous afternoon, which he personally had found the most difficult to accept. Not necessarily because David thought Cyril had lied about walking along this particular road as and when he had said, but in that Cyril had been sufficiently aware of his surroundings to notice that David's aunt, Margaret Sayer, was sitting in her living-room window watching him as he had walked past, and that he had then, further along the road, observed the two women cleaning up Roper's wall.

This was not the infuriatingly vague Cyril Forbes with whom ex-Detective Chief Superintendent Sayer had frequently crossed swords in the past; and up to a point, Mrs Charles had to agree with him. Regrettably, it was all part of the fiction that Cyril had set out deliberately to create about himself, that he walked about with his head up in the clouds, seeing nothing of what went on about him down here on Earth; whereas in reality, he was more observant, and astute, than the average person, though Mrs Charles knew that it would be a waste of time to try and convince David of this — or anybody else, for that matter. Cyril had done an excellent job; he was to be congratulated, she thought grimly. If he was to be sent down for this terrible crime — a crime which she had no doubt he had not committed — then no single person could have done more, metaphorically speaking, to slip the noose round his neck and spring the trapdoor beneath his own two feet than Cyril Forbes himself.

Mrs Charles paused suddenly at the side of the road and gazed thoughtfully across the open fields. Nobody had mentioned Stan North, where he was working yesterday . . . He could always be found, either out in the fields or crawling about in the hedgerows, looking for the bugs and hairy caterpillars he studied and observed as a guide for his weather forecasts. Even in the pouring rain. He surely must have seen Cyril yesterday . . .

She narrowed her eyes and continued to gaze into the distance, searching for some sign of human life crawling about on all fours in the fields. She gave a start as someone spoke her name; looked sharply at a clump of hawthorn growing raggedly several feet back from the verge on her immediate left.

'Oh, Mr North,' she said, as Little Gidding's unofficial weather forecaster and amateur entomologist straightened up from the half-crouching, half-crawling position he adopted while pursuing his hobby, and then stepped through the hedgerow and out onto the road. 'Good afternoon. You startled me.'

He raised his hat. 'Just wanted to say how sorry I am to hear about this bit of bother your brother's got himself into.'

'I'm afraid it's rather more than just a bit of bother, Mr North. Cyril's in quite serious trouble.'

'Yes,' he said, and nodded his head solemnly.

'I was hoping I'd see you.'

He nodded his head again. 'I thought you might be. I've been waiting for you. The police haven't got round to me yet, but they will, same as I knew you would sooner or later. I'm glad you found me first: I wouldn't want you to hear this second-hand. Wouldn't be right. I'd feel really bad about it.'

Mrs Charles's spirits sank a little. Stan North had, quite obviously, not seen Cyril during that crucial period of time around three o'clock the previous afternoon. 'Did you see my brother at all yesterday?'

He shook his head regretfully.

'Where were you working?'

'Out the back of the dairy. I could spend weeks there, in just that one spot.'

'How long did you spend there yesterday?'

He sighed. 'Now, that's a question.'

'You don't know how long you were there?'

He thought for a moment. 'I saw those two daft women, the pair of comedians with the buckets and mops who go round cleaning up the countryside, if that's of any use to you.'

'No, Mr North,' she sighed. 'I'm afraid not. That more than likely puts you in Roper's field when my brother says he was there. He too claims he saw Mrs Langston and Mrs Short cleaning up Mr Roper's wall.'

'That their names? I've often wondered,' he said musingly. 'Odd couple . . .'

She considered him for a moment, the khaki groundsheet he was wearing fastened round his shoulders like a *Batman* cape, and his battered hat with its bits of twigs and bird feathers sticking out of it, and wondered if it had ever occurred to him that people might be of the opinion that there was something a little odd about him, too. Margaret Sayer, who was one of Little Gidding's older residents, and whose late father had been the doctor there for most of his life, knew pretty well everything about everyone living in the village, and she claimed that it was Mrs North who had turned Stan's brain when she had run off with the insurance man who had called on her once a week.

'Did you work anywhere else yesterday?' Mrs Charles asked him at length.

He thought for a minute. 'I might've spent a bit of time in that wood down the bottom of your garden. Can't be sure, though, that it wasn't the day before.'

'Would that have been in the afternoon or the morning — can you remember that?'

'The afternoon, I think. But I'm not sure. Difficult to remember when you do the same thing day in day out, seven days a week. I probably wouldn't have even remembered exactly what day it was that I was in Roper's field if it wasn't for those two women with their buckets and mops.'

'And you're absolutely certain that you didn't see my brother?'

'Wasn't looking for him, was I?'

They lapsed into a thoughtful silence. Then Mr North said, 'Funny about that, Mr Forbes being out and about . . . It being a Wednesday and all. I haven't run into him out in the fields of a Wednesday . . . well, it must be a year or more since. He avoids everybody like the plague on Wednesdays now; shuts himself up in that oast-house of his where nobody can get at him . . .'

Yes, thought Mrs Charles as she continued alone slowly along the road: this was something everybody — everybody living in the village, that is — would know about Cyril. Judith Caldicott knew about it too, Mrs Charles suddenly recalled. Judith had wanted to call in on Cyril and say hello to him one Wednesday afternoon, and she (Mrs Charles) had had to explain to her that Cyril was always *incommunicado* on this particular day of the week. Had Judith remembered this and arranged to meet someone secretly at Cyril's place while Cyril was safely locked up outside in the oast-house? Or was she lured there to Cyril's isolated old farmhouse by her killer who knew this about Cyril, that it was a chance in a million that he would venture from the oast-house at all yesterday — morning, noon or night?

And yet that million to one chance had occurred. Against all the odds, Cyril had left the oast-house yesterday afternoon. Not to venture indoors — unfortunately for Judith — but to check out his computations in Roper's field. This should have ruined everything for her killer, destroyed his carefully laid plans completely; and yet it hadn't. His luck had held good for him because nobody saw Cyril.

Was this why Miss Sayer and Mrs Langston and Mrs Short didn't see Cyril —? Because they, like Stan North, hadn't expected to see him on a Wednesday?

Mrs Charles was approaching Miss Sayer's cottage and she paused for a moment and studied the road in relation to the window where Miss Sayer was always latterly to be seen sitting keeping a steady watch on everyone who passed her front gate. There was no doubt about it: the old lady had a perfectly clear view of the road, with or without the binoculars it was common knowledge that she kept well within hand's reach. There was no way she could have missed seeing Cyril as he walked past on his way to Roper's field. And the mere fact that it was Cyril — that he was out and about on a Wednesday — was, in itself, of sufficient noteworthy interest to ensure that she would not have missed taking in every detail of his progress along the road.

There was little point in asking herself why Miss Sayer would lie about something like this: the answer was all too obvious. Everybody in the village knew what Miss Sayer thought of Cyril Forbes: she had never made any secret of her contempt for him, that so far as she was concerned, he was a mental case, a menace to society.

Mrs Charles pondered for a moment. No one would deny that Miss Sayer was a vicious, spiteful old lady who spoke her mind with absolutely no thought for anyone's feelings and with precious little regard for the truth when it suited her; but would she be this spiteful, this vicious, towards someone who had never done her any harm other than to irritate her because he wasn't like other people and refused to conform?

Mrs Charles paused near Miss Sayer's front gate and gazed across the neatly laid out flower-beds at the very old, white-haired little woman sitting motionless in the living-room window. Miss Sayer stared back at her defiantly, then abruptly averted her head when a second person suddenly appeared in the window — Mrs Pendlebury, the late middle-aged widow who was taking care of Miss Sayer while she convalesced from a recent operation on her broken right femur. Mrs Charles could see that Mrs Pendlebury had brought Miss Sayer her afternoon tea.

Mrs Charles looked at her watch. It was five minutes to three.

She sighed and turned away; continued on into the village, pausing at the stone wall, responsibility for which the village dairy farmer and Gidding Town Council were currently disputing between them.

She could see the spotlessly clean patches which Mrs Langston and Mrs Short had left behind them yesterday afternoon, and when she went up to the wall, which was about five and a half feet high, and looked over it, as Cyril claimed Mrs Langston had yesterday afternoon, she had a clear view of the field. Or rather, of Mr Roper's herd of Friesian cows grazing in the field and drifting steadily towards the milking sheds.

Her information (courtesy of Stan North) was that she would find Mesdames Langston and Short cleaning up one of the road-signs near the village duck pond.

Mrs Short saw her coming and guessed her purpose. She spoke quickly to her companion and they looked at each other hesitantly, almost as if, thought Mrs Charles, they were debating whether or not to snatch up their cleaning equipment and make a run for it.

There was nothing at all odd, or even particularly remarkable, about the two women, aside from their obsession with the graffiti which, in common with so many parts of the countryside generally nowadays, was defacing their pretty, picture-postcard village and its environs. They were two, quite ordinary-looking, middle-aged housewives who had simply got fed up with waiting for somebody over there in the Town Hall to get up off their big fat backsides and do something positive about getting Little Gidding's (formerly) blank expanses of stone walling and road-signs stripped of their obscenities. The people of Gidding might be content to put up with confronting that sort of thing at every turn they made, the villagers of Little Gidding were not; and at least two of them were prepared to put their buckets and scrubbing-brushes where their mouths were and prove it.

Mrs Charles greeted them, then gave them both a friendly smile. 'I just wanted to say how sorry I am that you've found yourselves placed in this embarrassing situation over my brother, and to assure you that there are no hard feelings on either my part or his concerning the statements you've made to the police. You did what you had to. I would've done exactly the same thing had I been in your position.'

Mrs Short said, 'We're very sorry we couldn't help . . . I mean, that we didn't see your brother. We only wish we had, don't we, Pat?'

Mrs Langston agreed with her.

'What exactly did you see when you were cleaning Mr

Roper's wall yesterday?' asked Mrs Charles.

'How do you mean?' asked Mrs Langston. Her eyes narrowed defensively. 'We didn't see your brother.'

'Yes, I accept that, Mrs Langston,' said Mrs Charles. 'What I meant was, did you at any time while you were cleaning the wall, look over it into Mr Roper's field?'

'Well, yes, of course: I think so . . . I can't really remember for sure. Most of the time, though, I was bent over with my scrubbing-brush.'

'I can't see over the wall, so I didn't see anything,' said the diminutive Mrs Short, shaking her head adamantly.

Mrs Charles nodded; turned back to Mrs Langston. 'Can you recall what you saw when you looked over the wall?'

Mrs Langston looked puzzled. 'Just the field, the same as always.'

'What time would this have been?'

'We told the police all we know. We made a start on the wall soon after nine o'clock in the morning, and except for a short break at lunch-time, we were working there until a little after three o'clock — about three-thirty, wasn't it?' Mrs Langston asked her companion, who nodded quickly in agreement.

'Where were the cows when you left — in the milking sheds?'

'No, it was too early for that,' said Mrs Langston. 'They were still in the field . . . They're always there at that time of day. They come in on their own, don't they —? Towards milking time around four o'clock of an afternoon.'

'And they were definitely all there in the field when you looked over the wall, ready and waiting for their four o'clock milking?'

'Well, some of them were . . . I mean, I didn't actually take that much notice. I expected the cows to be there — well, they always are, aren't they . . . at that time of the day? — and there they were.'

Mrs Charles looked at Mrs Langston. 'Would it be possible that you glanced quickly over the wall sometime after lunch and mistook my brother for a cow moving in nearer to the milking sheds as the afternoon drew in?'

Mrs Langston looked affronted; frowned and shook her head. 'There's nothing wrong with my eyes, if that's what you're driving at. I don't wear glasses, and I don't need them, either. Besides, everybody knows Mr Forbes spends Wednesday locked up in his oast-house. He'd be the last person I'd expect to see in Roper's field on a Wednesday afternoon.'

Mrs Charles looked at her thoughtfully. 'Yes, I quite agree. Well, what about Mr North? Did you see him?'

Mrs Langston looked at Mrs Charles suspiciously. She had a feeling that this was a trick question, that Mrs Charles might be laying some kind of trap for her, and she tried to think up a response that would avoid the risk of her stepping into it. She looked at Mrs Short.

'What about you Mrs Short?' asked Mrs Charles, turning abruptly to her. 'Did you see Mr North at all yesterday?'

Mrs Short blinked, looked hard at Mrs Langston, then back at Mrs Charles. 'In Roper's field, you mean?'

'No, not specifically. Anywhere at all yesterday?'

Mrs Short looked back at Mrs Langston. 'I didn't see him, did you?'

Mrs Langston relaxed, felt it was safe now to commit herself. 'No, neither did I.'

CHAPTER FIVE

According to what little information David had been able to give Mrs Charles thus far, a total of four different people had seen Judith Caldicott drive through the village in her little bright red sports car at somewhere around two-forty-five the previous afternoon, and then continue along the road towards her (Mrs Charles's) semi-isolated bungalow. The two women cleaning up Mr Roper's stone wall, David's aunt, Margaret Sayer, and Tilly Cockburn, the cheerful, plump, middle-aged manageress of the Post Office Stores, who had spent the early part of her Wednesday afternoon off polishing the brass hardware on her front door.

Mrs Charles found Tilly, busy as usual, behind the counter in the grocery section of the Post Office Stores. Tilly was talking loudly over her shoulder to a woman customer about the grisly murder of the young pop star, and the increasing number of sex maniacs who Tilly claimed were everywhere one looked these days, and it was a moment or two before she realised, principally from the embarrassed hush that had suddenly descended upon the Post Office section of the store where a number of people were standing in line awaiting attention, that something was wrong. She flushed a bright scarlet when she turned quickly and caught sight of Mrs Charles.

'Oh, Mrs Charles!' she exclaimed. 'Forgive me, I didn't realise you were there; and anyway, you know I wasn't talking about Mr Forbes. I don't for one minute believe he had anything to do with Judith Caldicott's murder. He's not like that — I mean . . . well, you know what I mean . . .' She broke off, flustered, her colour deepening.

'It's all right, Tilly,' said Mrs Charles. 'I quite understand.

Please . . . you mustn't be embarrassed on my account.'

'Well, I am,' growled Tilly. She frowned crossly. 'Me and my big mouth! It's just that . . . well, seeing Judith the way I did yesterday when she went whizzing past in that snazzy little red car of hers, her lovely, long blonde hair streaming back from her face in the wind . . . I'll never forget it — that beautiful young girl, so full of life and with everything to live for, and not more than thirty minutes later, she was dead. It hits harder too when you've a girl of your own of the same age. You can't help looking at your own daughter and thinking to yourself, *My God, that could have been YOU!* Not that it would've been, what with Alison engaged and getting married Saturday week and all. Thank God she's safe now from all that sort of thing. When she goes out at night, I know exactly who she's with!'

While she finished serving her other customer, Tilly went on talking to both her and Mrs Charles about the agonies of being a parent today with all this permissiveness which she likewise claimed was everywhere one looked nowadays, but Mrs Charles wasn't really listening. She felt a deep sense of disappointment. While the time of death seemed fairly definite, she had been clinging to the slim hope that Judith might not have been murdered in her brother's living-room after all, that she had been killed elsewhere and had then been driven by her killer through the village and left in Cyril's house where her killer knew (or thought he knew) it would be some considerable time before her body was discovered. But with the hood of her car down, giving everyone a clear view of the young woman sitting behind the wheel, there could be no doubt about it: Judith had definitely driven her car herself through the village shortly before three o'clock yesterday afternoon and on to the bungalow, and then from there out to Cyril's farmhouse near the motorway.

'. . . And, of course,' Tilly was saying, 'having known Judith personally makes it even worse still. Alison hasn't stopped crying: she's going to make herself ill, the way she's carrying on. Den — that's Dennis Pendlebury, her fiancé —' Tilly glanced at Mrs Charles. 'You know Mrs Pendlebury, of course . . . she's been looking after Miss Sayer —'

Mrs Charles looked at her quickly. 'Alison was friendly with Judith Caldicott?'

Tilly nodded. 'Not so much recently — when they were at high school together in Gidding. They were best friends, inseparable. Then . . . well, you know how it is, boy-friends come along, and things are never quite the same then, are they? — and eventually they each went their own separate way. They haven't seen one another for years — not to talk to, I mean. They wouldn't have anything in common now, any-way. Alison has always been a bit of a homebody . . . only ever wanted to get married and settle down and have a home of her own and kids; whereas Judith — this was after her boy-friend died (he was killed on his motor bike some years back) — was determined to have a career, bright lights, and all the rest of it.'

'Do you know Judith's people at all?' asked Mrs Charles.

Tilly made a face. 'Wouldn't want to . . . Not judging by some of the things Alison used to come home from school with and tell me. Mrs Caldicott only used to wash up the dirty dishes once a week, when they'd finally run out of clean crocks and pans. Alison couldn't believe her eyes when Judith took her into their kitchen one day after school and she saw these great mountains of dirty dishes stacked up everywhere she turned. She talked of nothing else for days afterwards . . .' Tilly paused. 'That and the way they all fought with each other, like cat and dog. Alison said it was terrible the way they used to speak to one another. Judith wanted her to spend a weekend with her and her family once, but Alison got me to make up some excuse for her. In fact, she made herself quite ill about it. That was how much she didn't want to go . . .'

'She's upstairs in her bedroom bawling her stupid eyes out,' announced Master Richard Cockburn, opening the front door to his sister's fiancé, Dennis Pendlebury. 'The sooner you two get hitched and you put an end to her pre-nutral —' (*'nuptial'* being a word which had only recently been added to Richard's vocabulary, and never having seen it written down, he gave it his own faulty pronunciation) '— nerves, or whatever it is that Mum reckons she's got, the better,' the boy grumbled. 'Tell her to put a sock in it, will you?'

Dennis went upstairs and knocked on Alison's bedroom door. He had come straight from work, and was still in his greasy motor mechanic's overalls. He was employed by Jack Graves (the *& Son* of Graves & Son, Family Butchers) who also owned the local garage, which adjoined the butcher's shop, and who, in fact, preferred motor car engines to sides of beef, lamb and pork and spent more time working alongside Dennis than he did in the shop next door with his father.

Alison gazed at Dennis tearfully as he came into the room. He was twenty-two, a year older than she was, pleasant-looking (although a little on the short side) and nice enough, but rather stodgy and completely lacking in humour, the rest of the boisterous, happy-go-lucky Cockburn family thought. Just right for Alison, in other words.

'Hell's bells, Alison,' murmured Dennis when he saw her face, the red blotches covering her cheeks and the puffiness round her eyes. 'You're going to finish up really ill if you don't pull yourself together soon.'

'I can't help it. I keep thinking back and remembering how it used to be between us . . .'

'*Kissy, kissy, kissy!*' said a giggling voice through the crack in the open door.

'*I'll kill you, Richard Cockburn!*' Alison screamed at her brother.

Dennis got up and closed the door to prevent the eleven-year-old from saying anything further to upset his sister. He turned back to her. 'Look,' he said, 'I'll go home and get cleaned up, and then I'll drive you over to see Mr and Mrs Caldicott and you can have a talk to them about Judith. Would that make you feel any better?'

'I don't want to talk to them. I can't, you know I can't. He'll be there.'

He looked puzzled. 'Who do you mean?'

'I've told you. That horrid man — Judith's uncle. He lives

with them.' She burst into a fresh flood of tears. 'I can't talk to them with him there. I'm frightened to . . . He knows the truth: I'm sure he knows!'

Dennis sighed; shook his head. 'I wish I understood what's got into you, Alison. I think you're being very silly about this.'

'You forget . . . She was my best friend.'

'But that was years ago. I thought you told your mother that you couldn't even remember the last time you spoke to her.'

'It doesn't matter; she was still my best friend.'

'Anyone would think you killed her,' he remarked, his tone becoming a trifle impatient.

Alison started to sob. Her voice rose hysterically. 'But that's just it. Anyone who knows something and doesn't do anything about it is as guilty as the person who really killed her!'

He looked at her. 'What are you talking about? They've got the man who killed her.'

'No, they haven't. They've arrested an innocent man; I know they have! Oh, Dennis,' she sobbed. 'Why did this have to happen now; when I was so happy and everything was so wonderful? I'm so frightened. I've got to talk to someone about this.'

He sat down on the edge of the bed beside her; shook his head helplessly at her heaving shoulders; frowned. 'I can't help you, Alison. I'm sorry; this is something you've got to sort out for yourself.'

'I know,' she whispered in a choked voice. 'Oh, God,' she moaned into her hands. 'Please tell me I'm wrong.'

Alison was sitting at her dressing-table writing something down on a notepad when her brother, Richard, came upstairs a short while after Dennis had left to go home and change out of his working clothes.

'What do you want?' she asked him, quickly turning the notepad over as he came into her room so that he couldn't see what was written on it.

'Mum just phoned. You're to start getting tea ready, she

said. She's going to be late home tonight. She's going to do some shelf-filling or something; I'm hungry,' he finished, all in one breath.

'Greedy pig,' his sister sniffed. She scowled at him. 'Get something yourself. I'm not your slave.'

He sidled up to the dressing-table. 'Who are you writing to?'

'None of your business,' she said, pushing the notepad into the top drawer of her dressing-table and then sitting with her back hard up against it.

He started to fiddle with the things on the dressing-table and she slapped his wrist hard. He howled and doubled over, thrust his hurt wrist and hand between his knees and hobbled in circles round her room in an impressively noisy but pathetically poor imitation of someone genuinely suffering from intense pain, then staggered out through the door and tore down the stairs, raucously singing at the top of his voice, 'Alison's got a secret lover; *kissy, kissy, kissy*; she's upstairs writing mushy letters to him; I'm going to tell Dennis!'

Alison burst out onto the landing. 'I am not writing a letter! There, if you must know what I was doing . . .' A sheet of notepaper floated down onto Richard's head and he made a wild grab for it.

'What are all these names?' he asked, looking at it.

'Well, miracle of miracles,' she sneered down at him. 'The greedy pig can actually read! It's the guest list for my wedding, cloth-head.'

Richard looked at it again. 'Where's my name?' he demanded. 'It's not there.'

'Yes, and I'd think on about that if I were you, Richard Cockburn. It's my wedding, you know; and I'll have just who I want there!' His sister glared at him for a moment, then turned and swept majestically back into her room and slammed the door behind her.

CHAPTER SIX

Mrs Charles handed David his coffee and frowned to herself. He had something on his mind, something he was still debating whether or not to tell her.

He had given her what information he could on the Caldicotts, which wasn't a great deal, and which did little more than to confirm what Tilly Cockburn had told her the previous afternoon when she had called into the Post Office Stores. The Caldicotts were not a particularly pleasant family: no one that David had talked to about them, seemed to have a good word for any of them. P.C. Michael Caldicott was liked least of all. They were aggressive, quick to see a slight where none was intended, always on the defensive: Mrs Caldicott was on extremely bad terms with her immediate neighbour with whom she squabbled constantly, and had more than once called out the police to settle their disputes, among the most recent of which was one involving their sacks of household refuse and where they should not be left on the footpath outside the two houses for the Town Council's dustmen to collect.

P.C. Caldicott was twenty-five, fifteen years younger than his brother with whom he had lived since he was a small boy. He spoke often to his fellow police officers of his niece, Judith, and strongly disapproved of Ben Shipwell, who had been both her live-in lover and road manager, and who was also a member of her backing group, *Toy*. P.C. Caldicott claimed that Shipwell was a cocaine user, and boasted frequently that it was only a matter of time before he had the hard evidence to get Shipwell sent down for a very long time for drug pushing.

There was little else that David could tell Mrs Charles about the family other than to make the comment that there was about as much chance of P.C. Caldicott nabbing Shipwell, or anyone else for that matter, for drug pushing, as there was of his (David's) taking up needle-point classes!

At length, Mrs Charles put aside her coffee-cup and said, 'Well, Superintendent: are you going to tell me what it is that's bothering you?'

He scowled at her a little and said, 'I'm afraid to, afraid of what you'll say. I very much fear that it's going to put the lid on it for your brother.'

She looked at him thoughtfully; waited for him to continue.

'Where was he on Tuesday?'

She looked at him. 'Tuesday?'

David said, 'Remember what I told you yesterday . . . We've got to be honest between ourselves.' He paused. 'He was over in Gidding, wasn't he?'

'Yes . . . Why?'

'On Tuesday afternoon, the Gidding police got a phone call from the Caldicotts' neighbour — the one I was telling you about, the one Mrs Caldicott likes squabbling with. Apparently Mrs Caldicott had accused her — or rather, one of the neighbour's lads — of pinching a black lace brassiere belonging to Judith from off the washing-line to flog to one of his mates down at the local pub, and this time the neighbour was getting in first. She denied the charge, said nobody in her family went anywhere near the Caldicotts' washing-line, and wanted to make a charge of her own against Mrs Caldicott for defamation of character.'

'I see,' said Mrs Charles. She nodded her head slowly. 'This, I take it, is the black bra that was found tied round Judith's throat.'

'Yes. Her mother has identified it positively as being the one that was pinched from off the washing-line the day before. Merton wasn't sure until then that Judith hadn't been wearing it the day she was murdered. As I've told you, she was only partly-clothed; her upper garments had all been removed from her body. Mrs Caldicott told Merton that Judith seldom wore a bra (she was apparently particularly proud of that part of her anatomy!), and that she had no need of wearing one for support.' David hesitated. Then he said, 'Merton's lads are out looking for eye witnesses now, someone who can put your brother anywhere near the Caldicotts' semi on Tuesday afternoon. I don't know if you noticed it while we were over there yesterday, but there's a stretch of wooded ground running along the back of the house, so it's quite probable that whoever pinched the bra, slipped into their garden that way and wasn't seen by anybody. The back garden's pretty much like the rest of the place, I understand. A tip. The lawn is something between four and five feet deep and still growing while Mr Caldicott gets round to doing something about getting his lawn-mower fixed. That's another thing the Caldicotts are squabbling with their neighbours about. The neighbours claim the place is crawling with poisonous snakes that come up from the wasteland and search in the grass for field mice.'

Mrs Charles sighed.

'Would you have any idea at all if your brother was in that part of town on Tuesday?'

'I don't honestly know. Quite possibly.'

'I suppose he was on that noisy motor bike of his . . . wearing his purple crash-helmet and the black leather jacket with the white sunburst on the back of it?'

'Unfortunately, yes. I'm afraid we must face it: he's going to be only too easily remembered.'

The telephone rang. Mrs Charles looked at it for a moment, then turned to David and said, 'Would you mind answering that for me, please? The newspapers are becoming something of a nuisance. I'd rather not speak to anybody right now.'

He picked up the receiver; almost immediately began speaking rapidly into it. The call was for him; from his wife, '*Jean*,' he mouthed to Mrs Charles.

'He's there with you now?' David asked his wife after a few moments. Then: 'No, tell him to come straight over here: I'm sure Mrs Charles won't mind talking to him in the circumstances.'

'I hope you'll forgive the liberty,' David said to Mrs Charles as he rang off, 'but I've asked a young friend of mine — a newspaper reporter, I'm afraid — to come on over and see you. He told Jean he spoke to you on the phone last evening and you refused to talk to him.'

'I don't think I've got anything to say to the Press, Superintendent.'

'I dare say: but I think this young man's got something to say to you . . . To us.'

John Stanton had just turned twenty, and his job on the Gidding *'Daily Sketch'* was his first and very important to him; he was extremely enthusiastic and eager to make good, David explained to Mrs Charles while they waited for the young man to drive over to the village from town. He had been something of a tearaway in his early teens, and eventually had been caught by the police while he had been unwittingly driving a stolen car. It was a first offence, and David, a friend of the family, had pulled a few strings, and all charges against the lad had been dropped. The shock of his arrest and the intense distress it had caused his parents, had cured the young man for good of all future criminal intent, and he and the Sayers had since become close enough for him to look upon them as an honorary aunt and uncle.

He arrived half an hour later. He was extremely tall; had long gangly legs and arms that seemed to go on forever and with which he seemed to be uncomfortable and, from the moment he stepped through the front door, managed to wrap around everything he strayed too near. As a consequence, he spent a lot of his time red-faced and apologising. Mrs Charles liked him instantly, and regretted her abruptness with him over the telephone the previous night. He, in turn, was so overwhelmed by her change of heart towards him that, as David introduced them, he lunged forward to shake her hand, got his feet caught up in the handle of a brass coal-scuttle, fell into the fire-place and temporarily semi-disappeared up the chimney.

Safely installed, at length, in an easy chair that was a good arm and leg's distance from anything he could demolish, the young man explained the reason for his visit to Jean Sayer that morning.

'I thought you'd like to know, Uncle David,' he explained. 'It seemed a bit strange to me, and I knew that you and Mrs Charles were good friends; and when I was told I had to sit on the story for the time being, I thought that you, at least, ought to know —'

'All right, lad,' David interrupted him, his tone patient, although he felt anything but. 'Let's have it.'

'The *'Sketch'* had a phone call from one of the Caldicotts' neighbours and I was sent over there to interview her — a middle-aged woman with two teenaged boys . . . Baldwin is their name. There's a lot of bad feeling between them and the Caldicotts . . . one of the reasons the paper's backing off for the present until they — the paper, that is, has clarified the position, where it stands. The Baldwins wanted money, of course, for their story, and the Caldicotts, when my editor got on to them for verification of what I'd been told, threatened to sue the paper and the Baldwins if one word of any of it appeared in print. Anyway, according to what Mrs Baldwin told me, Judith Caldicott had a visitor on Wednesday morning soon after her mother left for work . . . That chap she lives with in London — Shipwell, Ben Shipwell — the lead guitarist in her backing group. Mrs Baldwin saw him arrive, then she nipped upstairs to her bedroom (Mr and Mrs Baldwin's bedroom is on the other side of the party wall to the room that Judith had been using since she came home) with a wine glass — the woman didn't mind admitting it! — and held it against the wall, then put her ear up to it and listened to what went on between them. Judith had got out of bed to answer the door to Shipwell, she claims. Judith and this guy made love — Mrs Baldwin reckons she heard it all through the wall! — then all of a sudden, they started to fight. Not physically, just yelling and screaming at one another at the top of their voices. The general gist of their row was that Judith was to go back to London with Shipwell then and there or he swore he'd break her neck. He's made her what she was; she owed him not to walk out on the group and leave them stranded high and dry.

'They're quite ordinary, you know,' the young man inter-
polated abruptly. '*Toy*, that is. Groups like them are two a
penny, here today and gone tomorrow. Ben Shipwell
might've made Judith, but she made him, his group; they were
quits, so far as I'm concerned. However, that's by the by. A
couple of hours later — Judith and Shipwell were yelling at one
another for most of this time — he stormed out of the house
and got into his car and drove off.'

'What about Judith?' asked David.

'Mrs Baldwin claims she heard her getting back into bed
and swears she stayed there until a short time before she went
out in the afternoon. Mrs Baldwin said Judith came out of the
house and got into her car and drove away at around about
two-fifteen.'

David nodded at Mrs Charles. 'That would give her half an
hour to get over to the village, which is about right.' He
looked back at the young man. 'Did Shipwell return during
the day?'

'Not so far as Mrs Baldwin knows.'

'What's that supposed to mean?'

'Well, she reckons somebody's been hanging about in those
trees at the back of their place — mostly at night, but once or
twice during the day — since Judith came home. One of the
Baldwins' lads spotted somebody one night and gave chase —
never caught up with anybody — and Mrs Baldwin thinks she
might've seen somebody one afternoon skulking about out
there while she was standing at the kitchen sink peeling the
vegetables for their evening meal.'

'Ben Shipwell?' asked David.

'She's not sure who it was,' replied the young man.

'Didn't anyone think to report this to the police?' asked
David.

'I asked her that, and she said they didn't really think much
about it until after what happened to Judith on Wednesday
afternoon. Then they sat down and started to work it out . . .
when they first noticed this peeping Tom, and how it could all
tie in with Judith's return home. That patch of common
ground is a notorious haunt for sexual perverts. The paper's

had complaints from quite a number of its readers at various times about there not being more policing of the area both during the day and at night.'

He looked expectantly from David to Mrs Charles. Neither made any comment. They were both thinking the same thing. It was all very interesting: in all probability there had been someone hanging about out the back, some sex pervert watching what went on in the bedrooms at the rear of the houses which backed onto the common ground, and in which, because these bedrooms were not overlooked by other houses, curtains were probably seldom ever drawn. Unfortunately, that someone could just as easily have been Cyril Forbes as Ben Shipwell. This piece of information was as damning for Cyril as was everything else, possibly more so. Particularly if Cyril's visit to Gidding on Tuesday had taken him anywhere near the Caldicotts' home and somebody remembered seeing him in the neighbourhood. And with the luck that Judith's killer seemed to be having, thought Mrs Charles grimly, this was a certainty. Like everything else that had gone wrong for Cyril, it was only a matter of time . . .

CHAPTER SEVEN

David stood at the sitting-room window watching John Stanton drive away.

'It gets worse by the minute, doesn't it?' he commented at length. He frowned as a woman bore down suddenly on Mrs Charles's front gate and then started up the path to the house. 'Oh Lord, now what? Here comes Mrs Pendlebury! I'll take care of it, if you don't mind. I think I can guess what this is all about.'

Mrs Pendlebury was an impressive-looking woman, tall, well-built, and with a briskly efficient, no-nonsense manner which the patients in her care claimed was annoying but secretly found immensely reassuring. She had married later than usual for her generation and her husband had died soon afterwards, leaving her with a young son, Dennis, to raise and support. It was then that she had resumed her former nursing career. She had taken an early retirement eight years ago from the post she had then held as matron of a geriatric nursing home, when her widowed, childless sister, Charlotte, had become terminally ill, selling up her own home and moving into her sister's bungalow in Little Gidding to care for her during her last days. Charlotte died the same year, and Mrs Pendlebury, recognising that her specialised nursing skills could be put to very good use in the village, which had a high proportion of elderly residents, and having been left the bungalow in which she and her son, Dennis, were living, had decided to remain in the village. There had been Dennis to consider, too. He had settled down far more quickly than she had expected after having lived in a busy, bustling town; and a matter of only a few weeks before Charlotte died, had been taken on by Jack Graves as an apprentice motor mechanic at his garage. Dennis told his mother that she could do as she wished, but he intended to remain in Little Gidding and, should she decide to leave, would seek lodgings with one of the villagers. He couldn't give up his new-found job, not when, out of seventy-two applicants applying from as far afield as Gidding, he was the lucky one to be given the apprenticeship. And besides, all his friends were in the village.

Mrs Pendlebury apologised to David for the intrusion. 'Your aunt simply insisted,' she went on. 'She spotted your car parked out on the road —'

Mrs Pendlebury hesitated; looked past David at Mrs Charles who had suddenly appeared in the hall. 'Oh, good morning, Mrs Charles: I'm very sorry to intrude on you like this, but I'm afraid Miss Sayer simply wouldn't take no for an answer.' Mrs Pendlebury looked back at David. 'Your aunt really would like to see you before you return home, Mr Sayer. I'd be obliged if you could spare her a few moments.'

David had a fairly shrewd idea that this meant his notoriously irritable aunt was rather more fractious than usual, and Mrs Pendlebury, competent and all as she was in dealing with the elderly, was beginning to weary of her, as would anybody exposed as remorselessly to her twenty-four hours a day as Mrs Pendlebury had been for the past month.

'Why don't you take the rest of the morning off,' he suggested to her, more out of pity for himself than for her. He couldn't bear to think of what he would do if Mrs Pendlebury washed her hands of his aunt and walked out on him. 'I'll sit with her for a couple of hours and give you a break.'

'That's very kind of you, Mr Sayer,' she said. 'I would appreciate it. There are a few things I'd like to pick up down in the village.'

'I'll drop you off,' he offered.

She shook her head. 'Thank you all the same, but I'd prefer to walk, if you don't mind. I feel I could do with a breath of fresh air.'

He appreciated her sentiments. He turned to Mrs Charles and said, 'I'll be in touch: you know where to find me if you need me;' and she nodded.

'Perhaps I could offer you a cup of coffee before you go down to the village,' Mrs Charles said to Mrs Pendlebury as David walked away from them.

Mrs Pendlebury looked surprised and flattered. She knew Mrs Charles only slightly, to greet whenever they passed one another in the village, and had often thought she would like to get to know her better.

'That would be very nice, thank you,' said Mrs Pendlebury, stepping inside.

'I've been hoping for an opportunity to have a word with you,' confessed Mrs Charles as they went through to the sitting-room.

Mrs Pendlebury nodded. 'About your brother, I suppose. I can't tell you how sorry I am about what's happened. It's all a dreadful mistake, of course; and don't you worry, my dear —' she patted Mrs Charles comfortingly on the hand '— the police will find that out soon enough. Mr Forbes has his funny little ways — it's no use pretending he hasn't; but everybody knows he wouldn't harm a fly. Believe me, I've dealt with enough people in my time to know who is and who isn't capable of murder! Things look pretty black for him now; I won't pretend they don't; but don't you worry, my dear. They'll find out who really killed that poor young girl.'

'I certainly hope so,' said Mrs Charles. 'I confess that I'm very concerned for Cyril. Miss Sayer's evidence is going to be particularly damning. I simply cannot understand why she didn't see him that afternoon.'

'No, neither can I,' said Mrs Pendlebury in a thoughtful voice. 'Miss Sayer must have seen him. I don't like saying this about one of my patients, but I can only think she's acting out of spite. She's certainly not senile; she's in full command of all her faculties — sharper I'd say, than most people half her age; so I can make no excuse for her on those grounds. She knows exactly what she's doing and saying.'

'Unfortunately, if she sticks by her story and gives evidence against my brother in court . . .' Mrs Charles didn't finish.

Mrs Pendlebury nodded sympathetically. 'You must be frantic with worry. I only wish there was some way I could help; but unfortunately, the more I try to discuss the matter with Miss Sayer, the more entrenched she becomes.'

'It's so very puzzling,' said Mrs Charles.

'My very words to her only this morning. And the real pity of it is that when I sat down and thought it over, I realised that it could only have been a matter of no more than a minute or two and I would've been in the living-room when your brother says he went past; and I'm sure I would've looked out of the window and seen him. It would've been Miss Sayer's word against mine. Though, of course, there's still Mrs Short — or was it Mrs Langston? I understand that your brother says he saw one of those ladies that afternoon, but she didn't see him.'

'Mrs Langston,' said Mrs Charles. 'My brother saw her looking over Mr Roper's wall.'

'Very odd,' said Mrs Pendlebury. 'I must say, though, that I'm surprised Mr Forbes noticed her. He doesn't generally notice people, does he? There have been quite a number of times that I've walked past him along the road, and in the village, and he's looked straight through me. I'm not implying any rudeness on his part, you understand: he simply hasn't seen me.'

Mrs Charles made no comment. Cyril was especially wary of widows; saw them coming a mile off!

'What exactly happened on Wednesday afternoon?' she asked Mrs Pendlebury. 'Was there anything at all out of the ordinary about any of Miss Sayer's behaviour — the things she said and did — that day?'

'No.' Mrs Pendlebury shook her head. 'That's what I find so very annoying. I did exactly the same thing I've done every afternoon since I've been caring for Miss Sayer. At a few minutes to three, I took in her tea to her, and a few minutes later I went back into the living-room to fetch her empty cup to wash it up. She drinks her tea very hot; I'm always warning her about it. I even warned her about it that afternoon. I think that was why she asked for a second cup, to annoy me because I'm always scolding her for drinking her tea too hot. She usually only has the one cup in the afternoon because I like her to have her evening meal at five o'clock, earlier than she normally has it, so that I can get finished up for the day . . . at least so far as meals are concerned. That leaves me with a fairly clear evening — I can sit and watch some television, or catch up on my knitting, until it's time for her cocoa and for me to get her ready for bed.'

'Did she say anything else to you — apart from asking for a second cup of tea, that is?'

'She mentioned the girl — Judith, Joujou . . . That was her name, wasn't it? Made some comment about her not wearing a scarf on her head. The top of her car was down, Miss Sayer said, and the girl's long hair was flying about all over the place. Getting in her eyes, Miss Sayer said. She said that it was a miracle the girl could see where she was going, and that it was small wonder there were so many nasty road accidents, what with people like her, that young girl, doing dangerously stupid things like that, and people hanging those silly little dog ornaments and trinkets on their rear-view mirrors and interfering with their vision. She was quite steamed up about all of it.'

'Did you see Judith drive past?'

'No, I was in the kitchen making the tea. Miss Sayer mentioned that she'd seen the girl when I took it in to her shortly before three o'clock.'

'If Judith saw my brother walking along the road that afternoon,' said Mrs Charles musingly, 'why on earth did she drive on to his place when she found that I wasn't in?'

'She obviously didn't see him,' said Mrs Pendlebury.

Yes, thought Mrs Charles wryly. That was just it: no one saw Cyril on the road that day; not even his alleged victim!

She wondered about Judith after Mrs Pendlebury had left, why Judith hadn't seen Cyril, and finally reached the conclusion that Judith was already inside his house with her killer when he came out of the oast-house and set off for Roper's field. The oast-house was behind the farmhouse proper, and Cyril would have come out of there, his mind full of his computations, and then cut across to the narrow, semi-secluded private lane which connected his property and an empty cottage (which was set even further back in the fields) with the main road into the village, without going anywhere near the front of the house where Judith would have parked her car. He wouldn't have been able to see her car from where he was: wouldn't have even seen it when he returned home that afternoon because he went straight back into the oast-house, using the same route as before, to do some more work on his computer. His house was not accessible directly from the main road, although it could be seen from there.

She frowned thoughtfully and posed the question she could no longer avoid asking herself. Which of them was lying? Miss Sayer or Cyril? They couldn't both be telling the truth. She didn't feel quite so concerned about the statement that Mrs Langston had made to the police. If she (Mrs Charles) could see the possibility that the woman (who by her own admission, would not have expected to see Cyril in Roper's field on a Wednesday afternoon in particular) could have mistaken Cyril for a cow when she glanced over the wall, then so could a good defence lawyer. But Miss Sayer was a very different matter. And she would not be shaken in her testimony, either. Knowing Miss Sayer as well as she did, the sharpness of her tongue, if anybody was going to be left shaken, it would be the defence lawyer! There was absolutely no doubt about it, she was going to make a very strong witness if the case against Cyril came to trial. Unless, in the meanwhile, Miss Sayer had second thoughts and was prepared to change her story and admit that she had seen Cyril that afternoon. The old lady, Mrs Charles was very much afraid, was really killing two birds with the one stone, brother *and* sister. Miss Sayer had no time for clairvoyants; would have been furious that the young pop star was consulting her; might even, in some strange, twisted way, consider the ends justified the means, that she was serving the public good by setting Cyril and Judith up as examples of the kind of misfortune that could befall those who were foolish enough (in her opinion) to have anything to do with fortune-tellers. Mrs Charles would not have wished to appear uncharitable towards the old lady, but the sad fact of the matter was that Miss Sayer would relish in her downfall, more so than in Cyril's.

She sighed. This was getting her nowhere. In fact, if she were to be truthful with herself, her investigations — and David's — were in this instance, as David had phrased it, *'putting the lid on it'* for Cyril. Screwing it down even more tightly. They were actually doing him more harm than good. Did this mean that the real killer was extremely clever, had everything planned to include her and David and their attempts to extricate her brother from the very serious trouble he was in? Had Judith's killer so arranged everything that the more she and David tried to get at the truth, the worse everything would seem for Cyril? Or was the killer simply endowed with more than an average amount of good luck? And if so, how long was it going to hold out for him? By the law of averages, sooner or later, the tide would turn . . . Something, she sighed again softly to herself, had to go right for Cyril.

CHAPTER EIGHT

'Of course that silly cat, Patricia Langston, wouldn't have seen him!' snapped Miss Sayer. 'She'd only have seen him if he'd had a big rude word painted down the front of him; and not even Cyril Forbes is that daft!'

Miss Sayer looked the picture of good health, despite her seventy-eight years and the frailness of her build. Her cheeks were the brightest of pinks (at the moment, admittedly, a little flushed with annoyance at her nephew, David's persistent obtuseness), and contrasted quite dramatically with the pure, snowy whiteness of her short, very curly hair which Mrs Pendlebury had trimmed and shampooed for her first thing that morning.

'Daft enough to say you saw him,' remarked David.

Miss Sayer looked at him, narrowed her slightly hooded grey eyes, then looked out of the window. Picking up the binoculars that were wedged down the side of her chair, she gazed fixedly at something for a moment or two and then tucked them away again.

'You're getting quite a reputation for doing that, spying on people all the time,' David growled at her.

'Just as well, isn't it?' she snapped. 'At least everybody knows who to come to when they want some good, solid, reliable information. Somebody round here has got to keep their eyes open and their wits about them.'

'You'll be called to give evidence, you know.'

She looked at him steadily; made no comment.

'It's not going to be very pleasant.'

'For whom: me, or for that fool up the road?' She looked at him for a moment, then gazed out of the window again. 'It's about time you and Edwina Charles got up off your backsides and did something before it's too late, isn't it?'

He looked puzzled. 'How do you mean?'

She didn't look at him; snorted through her nose. 'Any fool with half a brain could tell you that Forbes never killed that girl. He wouldn't have the wit!'

'Well, the way things stand, he's the one who's going to get sent down for it.'

'Nothing I can do about that!' she retorted.

'You're absolutely certain that you didn't see him on Wednesday afternoon?'

Miss Sayer's thin lips set firmly. She didn't reply.

David sighed. 'Isn't there at least a slight possibility that you didn't see him because you weren't expecting to see him? Everybody knows he stays put in the oast-house every Wednesday.'

'You didn't,' she reminded him.

'No, all right; I'll admit I thought he still skulked about in the fields all day Wednesday playing silly beggars the way he used to when I was on the Force. But I'm different: I don't live here in the village; I don't know Forbes as well as you do.'

Miss Sayer snorted; said nothing.

'He's in very serious trouble, you know.'

'I'm not senile,' she said. 'Not yet, anyway. I can still tell the difference between what's serious and what isn't.' She paused; narrowed her eyes at him. 'What's Mrs High and Mighty Charles got to say about all of this?'

He chose his words carefully: the old lady was antagonistic enough as it was. 'She thinks there's been a terrible mistake.'

'Yes, and I'm not the one whose made it, if that's what you're driving at!' She snorted again. 'What that girl needed to consult her for I'll never know.'

David fully realised that his aunt was inviting him to confide in her, but he was in no mood to become involved in a heated argument about the integrity of fortune-tellers, which was how it would all finish up. 'How did the girl look to you on Wednesday?'

'How do any of these young girls of today look? As if there

was nothing between her ears but a long cold draught, of course. How else?'

'Did she look happy, carefree; or worried and anxious?' He read the thought behind the look his aunt gave him. 'I know you only saw her for a few seconds, but you're usually pretty sharp about these things: you must have formed some impression of her.'

She looked at him, then a movement further along the road where she knew Stan North was working, caught her eye and she watched him for a moment or two.

'Where was that fool, Stan North, on Wednesday afternoon?' she asked, looking back at her nephew. 'Any of those useless individuals you've got posing as a police force over there in Gidding thought to ask that question yet?'

'Mrs Charles has had a word with him about it. He was in Roper's field.'

Miss Sayer made no comment.

'Well, was he?' asked David.

'I can't see Roper's field from here, can I? I can only see the road and who walks along it. And who doesn't!'

David sighed. 'All right, then . . . Was North working along the road, as he is now, at any time on Wednesday?'

'For a while, in the morning.'

'Not in the afternoon, around the time that Forbes said he came by here on his way to the dairy?'

'He was poking about in that wood at the bottom of Edwina Charles's back garden for most of the afternoon.'

'Before or after Judith Caldicott drove past here?'

'After.' The old lady looked at him impatiently. 'She would've seen him, wouldn't she? — if he'd been there at the bottom of Edwina Charles's garden when she went past here. She could've asked him if he knew where she could find Edwina Charles and then, for all we know, she might be alive today to tell the tale herself instead of lying dead on a cold mortuary slab.'

'The girl went round to the back of the bungalow?'

Miss Sayer looked at her nephew as if he were even more

feeble-minded than she had previously supposed. 'What else would she do when she couldn't get an answer at the front door? That woman was supposed to be expecting her, wasn't she?'

'Then what happened?'

'She came out and got into her car and drove on to Forbes's place the way I said.'

'And you're positive you saw nobody else?'

'Frank Blackmore went past, but that was earlier in the afternoon. He usually goes crawling over there on his hands and knees to Gidding to eat humbug-pie with that pompous old windbag, Selwyn Haycraft, on Wednesdays. He must've come back home through the village. I certainly didn't see him again that day. And Edwina Charles went down to the vicarage at two-thirty. She went home at four o'clock. But I've already told you all of this — and the police — a thousand times! You're not going to find your answers to who killed that girl in any of that lot, or by sitting there on your backside asking me a lot of daft questions.'

'Where would you look?'

'I'm not the one with the crystal ball, am I?' She looked at him for a moment, then turned her head and fixed her gaze on Stan North again. 'Plain as the nose on your face that somebody in the village knows something and isn't coming forward because they're shielding someone,' she said at length.

'It's a possibility,' he admitted. He looked thoughtful; raised his eyebrows at her meaningfully. 'There's also a possibility that someone knows something and is deliberately withholding that information from the police for some other deeply personal reason of their own. Or has seen something without realising its significance.'

'*Humph!*' she said; and then, after a slight pause: 'You'd better get cracking then, hadn't you? That's if it really matters to anyone in authority today whether or not somebody else is going to get themselves savagely attacked and murdered!'

CHAPTER NINE

Alison Cockburn hurried along the road past the old brewery. It was a chilly morning and she shivered inside her warm coat. Her eyes were red and puffy from crying — she was still sniffling — and she was late. The clock in St Stephen's bell-tower had already chimed the hour of six o'clock, and if the newspapers were on time and Mr Mortimer was downstairs in the shop, he would have already made a start on the sorting.

Her brother, Richard, cycled past her with his empty canvas paper-boy's delivery sack slung over his shoulder.

'You're going to catch it,' he called back over his shoulder to her, and wobbled about so dangerously that he almost lost control of his machine and had to put a foot on the ground and scoot along it vigorously until he came to a full stop and regained his balance.

She scowled at him. 'Serves you right.'

He leered at her. 'You're not *still* bawling? Just as well you're wearing a veil over your face next Saturday. You'll look like the bride of Dracula!'

Richard pushed off and disappeared round the corner. His sister was approaching the butcher's shop. There was a light showing on the window of one of the rooms in the living-quarters over the shop, and the garage next door, where her fiancé was employed, had been opened up, though it was much too early for Dennis to be there yet. He didn't start work until eight o'clock.

She knew who was in the garage and her heart thumped a little. He was always there when she went past of a morning; making his disgusting innuendoes about her and Dennis and their wedding night; pretending he was down there early working on the books. She knew why he was really there. He had grabbed her and kissed her full on the mouth once; said he only wanted to congratulate her on hearing that the wedding-date had been fixed. But it wasn't that kind of kiss, and her stomach churned a little at the memory of the manner in which he had suggestively pressed his pelvis against hers. Dennis said it was best to ignore him; that once they were married, he would leave her alone. It was disgusting, she thought; a man of his age — he would be at least her father's age, forty-three — still wanting to have sex! It made her feel sick; sicker, when she thought about that common little tart he was seeing behind his wife's back out there in that old cottage and she imagined them together, the things they would be doing with one another. She had told Carol what he was like; that she was a mug to think she was the only one: tried to make her see sense. What did Carol see in him? That was what she couldn't understand. He made her flesh crawl! It was about time somebody did something about it; told Mrs Graves what was going on and Mrs Graves put a stop to it.

Alison started to snivel again and, as she had expected, Jack Graves suddenly appeared in the doorway of the small reception office at the front of the garage. She quickened her step and moved further out onto the road; widened the gap between them. 'Not long now,' he called to her, smirking. 'Bet you can hardly wait, eh? Decided where you're going for your honeymoon yet?'

She forced her lips into a tight little smile; took Dennis's advice and ignored him.

She turned the corner. The lights were on in the news-agent's, and her brother and several of his friends were larking about outside on the footpath on their bicycles waiting to begin their rounds. She hoped Mr Mortimer hadn't finished sorting the papers — the ones for the houses along the road out to the motorway, anyway.

Mrs Charles didn't find a moment to sit down with her morning paper until shortly before eleven o'clock when she made herself a cup of coffee, principally because the delivery that morning had been considerably later than usual, and the telephone had rung almost constantly since soon after seven o'clock. Someone from the Gidding *'Daily Sketch'* rang (not David Sayer's young friend, John Stanton) wanting to know if she had anything to say about her brother who was going to be taken from the cells this morning and who would be appearing before the Magistrates' Court while the police made an application for his remand in their custody for seven days while they completed their inquiries. Mrs Charles had no comment to make other than to say that this was the first she had heard of it; then David rang moments after she had put down the telephone receiver and confirmed what she had been told. He also told her that the inquest into Judith Caldicott's death, which was scheduled for eleven-thirty on the following Monday morning, would be opened, but adjourned until a later date. There was, he said, very little point in either one of them attending it.

Anne Blackmore telephoned next with an apology for not having called round to see her to express, in person, the distress she and her husband, Frank, felt over Mr Forbes's predicament. Frank, she explained, intended to preach a special sermon at tomorrow's family service, the theme of which would be *'judge not lest ye be judged'*, or something along those lines, and prayers for Mr Forbes and Mrs Charles would also be said. Mrs Charles asked Anne to thank Frank on behalf of Cyril and herself, but hastened to add that so far as the vicar's sermon was concerned, everybody in the village had been most sympathetic towards her and her brother, not one unkind word had been said, certainly not to her face; to which Anne had responded, rather anxiously, 'Oh, I didn't mean to imply that we, Frank and I, think for one moment that Mr Forbes has done anything improper. There's absolutely no doubt in our minds that he's completely innocent. Someone's bound to remember having seen him on Wednesday afternoon . . . You just wait and see if I'm not right!'

This being the third day since the beautiful young pop star's murder, Mrs Charles no longer shared Anne Blackmore's optimism about a surprise witness. Someone would have come forward by now. Everybody knew how desperately urgent it was that she should find someone who had seen Cyril either walking along the road to Roper's dairy, or in the field with the cowherd. Wednesday afternoons were so very quiet in the village, this was the real problem: Little Gidding was not on the road to anywhere special, so even on a normal day, there was very little road traffic about; and generally speaking, once the shops closed for the day at one p.m. on a Wednesday, most people seemed to go indoors and stay there. There was, therefore, only the slimmest of possibilities that someone other than the two women Cyril had named, had seen him that afternoon; and if there were such a person, then he or she obviously had some very good reason of their own for keeping quiet about it.

The single sheet of notepaper — an advertisement for something or other, Mrs Charles thought at first — fluttered from between the pages of the morning paper as she opened it up to read it. She bent and picked up the piece of paper from off the floor, and taking a quick glance at the bold lines of printing centred on it, assumed that someone had sent her a poison pen letter. People were suddenly no longer being quite so charitably-minded about her brother, despite her assurances to the contrary to Anne Blackmore. Three times already that morning she had answered the telephone only to be abused by the anonymous callers (one man and two women) about her brother. She had no reason to suppose that any of the calls she had received had been made from within the village precincts: however, human nature being what it was, she knew that it would be naive of her to think that everyone in the village would be prepared to believe in her brother's innocence.

She frowned as she read what was printed on the piece of paper.

ASK JUDITH'S UNCLE ABOUT THE MOTOR BIKE. HE KNOWS THE TRUTH ABOUT WHO KILLED HER.

A green, felt-tip pen had been used to write the note, and some of the heavy inking was smeared, as if droplets of water had splashed on it accidentally, either while the note was being written or afterwards as its author had read back through it.

It was a pathetically inept attempt at anonymity: Mrs Charles guessed immediately who had sent her the note. The ink smears confirmed it. Alison Cockburn had sent it to her — Alison, who worked for Mr Mortimer in the newsagent's shop in the village and part of whose job it was to sort the newspapers early each morning ready for the paper-boys to deliver. And as Alison had written the note, she had been weeping so heavily, her tear-drops had fallen onto the notepaper. Mrs Charles clearly recalled Alison's mother, Tilly, mentioning a motor bike during the conversation she'd had with her in the Post Office Stores on Thursday morning — an accident which had resulted in the death of one of Judith's early boy-friends — and that Alison was extremely upset about Judith's murder, abnormally so considering that they were no longer the close friends they had once been during their high school days, and in tears most of the time.

With an overwhelming sense of relief, Mrs Charles went and got her coat and set off for the village. This was the break she had been hoping for, the break she had feared wouldn't come in time to keep her brother out of prison. Alison Cockburn knew something . . .

The colour drained from Alison's face and left her chalk-white when she turned from the magazine rack she was tidying and saw Mrs Charles coming through the doorway of the shop. She could tell by the look in Mrs Charles's eye that she had guessed about the note, she knew who had sent it to her.

Defensively, the girl got quickly behind the counter, looked at Mrs Charles fearfully, then glanced nervously behind her to see whether Mr Mortimer was watching her. He was talking to somebody on the telephone about an extension he was thinking of having built onto the back of the shop. His gaze was fixed on the notepad on which he was jotting down a series of figures.

Alison spoke first. Her eyes were brimming with tears.

'Please . . . I know why you've come . . . I can't say anything to you here. Oh, please . . . not now —' she glanced nervously at her employer again '— please go away; I'm in enough trouble with Mr Mortimer as it is for being late for work this morning.'

'When can we talk, Alison?' asked Mrs Charles, lowering her voice so that Mr Mortimer wouldn't hear what she said.

Alison moistened her lips; flicked her eyes anxiously at the man speaking on the telephone. 'This afternoon . . . I have to go and see Mrs Blackmore about the floral arrangements for my wedding next Saturday. I'll come and see you afterwards. I promise . . .' She looked at Mrs Charles, her chin quivering tremulously.

'Very well, Alison. I'll be expecting you.'

'I promise I won't forget,' said the girl. She hesitated. 'You won't tell anybody about this, will you? Mum'll kill me if she finds out what I've done. Promise you won't tell.'

Mrs Charles nodded. 'But you must keep your word and come and talk to me this afternoon.'

'I will,' the girl assured her, casting another anxious glance in Mr Mortimer's direction as he prepared to ring off.

He was putting down the telephone receiver as Mrs Charles turned and walked out. He was in a bad mood. The figures he had been quoted for the work he wanted done to his premises put the whole idea right out of court. If he couldn't get somebody else to give him a considerably lower quotation, he would have to forget all about it for the present, perhaps for even a year or more, which was most annoying. Perhaps he would drive over to Gidding in the afternoon and see that chap he'd been introduced to that time . . . One of these cowboy builders, but fairly reliable. Then he remembered. He'd promised that wretched girl she could take the afternoon off; he'd have to stay here and take care of the shop.

He looked at Alison sourly. 'What was that all about? Another complaint about the late delivery of the papers this morning? You're going to have to pull your socks up, young lady, if you're going to continue working for me after you're married. I can't be doing with staff making a convenience of me . . . flitting off here, there and everywhere when the mood takes them . . . coming in late, or not at all. You're going to have to sort yourself right out. Jobs don't come two a penny these days, you know. Nobody's indispensible —'

CHAPTER TEN

Jack Graves watched Alison Cockburn from the window of the reception office of his garage. He had been waiting for some minutes for her to come out of the newsagent's shop. She was running late, which was a damned nuisance. That miserable, penny-pinching old grouch, Mortimer, he expected. It would be just like Mortimer to go out of his way deliberately to find things for the girl to do and hold her up.

Alison didn't look his way once, but he had a feeling that she knew he was watching her. She had crossed the road and was walking quickly towards the dairy. Thanks to Dennis, he knew that she was going to the vicarage; that she and the vicar's wife and one or two of the flower ladies would be going over to the church this afternoon to decide on the floral arrangements for the wedding next Saturday . . .

His eyes followed her along the road. He wouldn't leave just yet awhile: he would wait a few minutes longer; give her a good head start; wait until she had gone past the dairy and disappeared around the corner into the road out to the motorway before making a move. Then by the time he had got to the brewery, she should be just about ready to turn off down the lane to the vicarage.

He turned his head and craned his neck so that he could look through one of the small internal windows and into the workshop. He could see Dennis's legs and feet poking out from beneath the car he was working on.

A minute and a half later, Graves left the garage by a small rear door which gave out onto a cobbled courtyard on which a number of motor vehicles, including the butcher's van, were parked. As he crossed the courtyard, he glanced up quickly at one of the windows at the rear of the butcher's shop, but the curtains were still tightly drawn and no one was watching him. Sylvia had gone upstairs to lie down soon after lunch. The cold bitch had one of her migraine headaches; probably wouldn't stir herself for the rest of the day. And if she did, if she came down to the garage looking for him, which wasn't terribly likely . . . well, that would be no problem. Dennis was a bit thick about some things, but he knew the score: he was a good lad; he'd cover for him as usual.

Alison hurried past Miss Sayer's cottage. She kept her head down; couldn't bring herself to look and see if she was being watched. Her chest felt as though it were clasped in an iron fist. Why people put up with that horrible old woman was more than she could understand. She hated her, really hated her; always watching every move she made, spying on her; making snide remarks about the young girls of today — meaning *her*, of course. She could feel her eyes on her now, burning two big holes in the middle of her back.

The afternoon was drawing in, growing dark earlier than usual because of the heavy black rain clouds that were banking up threateningly overhead. A wind had sprung up, and it was growing very chilly. Alison was shivering: she had been shivering all day, and soon after lunch, had developed a particularly sore throat. It was all this worry, getting so upset about everything — the wedding and all — and fretting about that poor Mr Forbes going to prison, and what people would think of her for not speaking out sooner: it had lowered her resistance, and she was certain it was her turn now, she was in for a bad dose of the Gidding flu. She should've known she'd finally come down with it. She and Richard were about the only ones who hadn't caught it.

She shivered quite violently; felt nauseated. She had been feeling sick for days, ever since she had heard about Judith and she knew she was going to have to make up her mind and do something about it. Her head started to ache. She wondered if she ought to say something to Mrs Blackmore; if she should tell her that she was—

She gave a start and looked round quickly as she heard a car turn off the road she had been walking along a minute or two earlier. She stepped over onto the verge and paused; waited. Her heart skipped a beat; felt as though it was turning cartwheels. She knew whose car it was; knew who would be sitting behind the wheel; knew he would have seen her leaving work for the vicarage; knew that he was watching her closely now, every move she made; knew that the car would stop and that she would be offered a lift the rest of the way up to the vicarage.

Should she accept it? Which was the best way to handle this?

It started to rain heavily and she quickly unfurled the long black umbrella she was carrying. She shivered fitfully as she waited for the car to reach her; looked anxiously about her. *It was so dark and lonely here!* In the distance, she could see lights shining on the vicarage windows; but would anybody hear her from as far away as this if she cried out . . . in all this wind and rain? And did she want that embarrassment, the Blackmores — and those tittle-tattling flower ladies, perhaps — running out to see what was the matter and then having to explain to everybody what had been going on? There was Dennis to think of, too: she couldn't make a fool of him by behaving like a silly, hysterical child over this. She was a grown-up woman now, old enough to be married: it was time she stood on her own two feet. This was her problem: she should have faced up to it ages ago; at least told her mother and asked her advice before things got so dreadfully out of hand like this.

The car was slowing. It drew up and the door on her side opened. She had to wait a moment while a sheet of hardboard was moved from the passenger-seat and into the back. She couldn't think what that was doing there; it seemed a strange thing to be carrying around in someone else's car. Then she closed her umbrella, shook it a little to shed its moisture, and climbed in beside the driver. They were only a couple of minutes' drive from the vicarage. He wouldn't be so silly as to try anything here.

★   ★   ★

Dennis scowled as the telephone, which he had been determined to ignore until he had finished what he was doing, continued to ring.

'Where the hell was Graves?' he muttered to himself. 'He should've been back ages ago.' He screwed himself round so that he could see the electric clock on the wall and was surprised to find that it was going on for five-thirty, much later than he had thought.

He dragged himself out from under the car on which he had hoped to get a lot more work done before knocking off time that evening, and then, wiping his hands on an oily rag, crossed to the reception office and picked up the telephone receiver.

'Graves's Garage,' he intoned.

It was Mrs Graves telephoning from her bedroom next door. He had more than half-expected it would be her; that was why he had finally decided that he had better answer the call. 'No, I'm sorry, Mrs Graves: Mr Graves still isn't back. He's delivering Mr Jackson's car to him. Yes, I know it's getting late, but he shouldn't be long now.' The young man sighed to himself; listened patiently for several moments to the monotonous whine coming from the woman complaining to him at the other end of the line. Then he said, 'Yes, Mrs Graves; but that was only the test run. You know Mr Graves likes to be sure everything's okay before delivering a car back to a customer. And you know the trouble Mr Jackson always gives us. There's always something he can find to complain about.'

Dennis reaffirmed that he was sure it would be only a matter of fifteen minutes at most before Mr Graves returned: then, sighing again, he rang off. He didn't wonder that Graves chased after other women; that woman drove him to it: but things were definitely getting a bit sticky. He'd warned Graves when he'd sneaked off on Wednesday afternoon that he was pushing his luck: Mrs Graves was suspicious and definitely on the warpath; she knew there was something funny going on. She'd never phoned the garage twice like this before. Mr Graves and he were going to have to make very sure they got their stories straight tonight when he got back otherwise there'd be trouble. Big trouble!

Mrs Charles checked the time again. It was now twenty minutes to six. Alison wasn't coming. The obvious explanation for her not turning up as promised, was the sudden change in the weather, but Mrs Charles felt uneasy about it. She had grown doubtful that Alison would genuinely know anything about Judith's murder that might help Cyril's case, but now she wondered; and if she was wrong and Alison did know something that would confirm the prophecy of the Tarot — the persistent warning of an ever-present threat to Judith's life arising, in all probability, from some incident that had taken place in the past — then there was a very definite risk that her life was now in similar jeopardy and from the same source. She had probably gone straight home from the vicarage when the weather had taken a turn for the worse, but Mrs Charles decided not to wait any longer and to contact Anne Blackmore and make sure that the girl was safe.

'She had a very sore throat and the shivers all day and finished up having to cancel her appointment with me this afternoon,' Anne explained in response to Mrs Charles's query as to Alison's whereabouts. 'I only hope it's a straightforward cold and not that wretched Gidding flu that's been flattening everybody for the past couple of weeks. It would be a pity if she's ill for Saturday. Anyway, her father said she's tucked up warmly in bed and taking plenty of hot drinks, so with a bit of luck she'll be fine again by then.'

'I'm sorry, I think I might've misunderstood you,' said Mrs Charles. 'Are you saying that Alison didn't come to the vicarage at all today?'

'Yes, that's right. Mr Cockburn phoned me a few minutes before she was due to arrive and told me she wasn't well and that she couldn't make it today . . . we'd have to go ahead without her.'

Mrs Charles hesitated; frowned to herself. 'It was Mr Cockburn who phoned you; you're sure of that?'

'Yes, of course I'm sure.'

'You recognised his voice?'

There was a pause. Then Mrs Blackmore said, 'I don't understand . . . There's something wrong, isn't there? Oh Lord, you don't think something's happened to Alison, do you?'

'I hope not, Mrs Blackmore.' Mrs Charles hesitated. Then she said, 'I don't suppose the man you spoke to had a husky voice by any chance?'

'Well, yes, it was a bit husky. He said he'd got a cold — just about everyone in the village seems to have got a dose of that wretched Gidding flu, or they're coming down with it; and he thinks he's probably given it to Alison. He said the whole family's been ill with it, one after the other. And I know for a fact that Tilly was complaining of a sore throat one day last week.' There was a slight pause. Then Anne said, 'I can appreciate how you must be feeling after what's happened to Judith Caldicott, but I'm quite sure there's nothing to worry about. Alison must've forgotten to tell her father that she was calling round to see you after she left me.'

'Yes, probably,' said Mrs Charles. 'Still, I think I'll get in touch with her father and make sure she's all right, just to be on the safe side.'

'It wouldn't hurt,' agreed Anne. 'Will you let me know? I feel a bit concerned about this now . . .'

Mrs Charles got in touch with Mr Mortimer the newsagent first; asked to speak to Alison. She hoped and prayed that she was wrong, but as expected, he told her that Alison wasn't there: she had taken the afternoon off to see Mrs Blackmore about the flowers for her wedding; had left the shop soon after three o'clock. She was running a bit late, he explained. Her own fault. She had been late in arriving for work that morning, and the least she could've done, bearing in mind that she wasn't being docked for her afternoon off, was to make sure that she was on time in the morning. These young girls who no sooner they left school and started work, got themselves engaged to be married, were more trouble than they were worth . . .

Next, Mrs Charles telephoned Graves's Garage. Mr Mortimer had told her that all the lights were on, and that so far as he knew, young Pendlebury was still somewhere about the place.

Dennis was on the point of locking up when the telephone started ringing. Mrs Graves again, he thought. He didn't know what he was going to say to her this time. *That her husband had phoned in to say he'd broken down somewhere?* No, too dangerous. What would happen if Graves went straight indoors to her when he got back and told her some other yarn? The fat would really be in the fire then, all right!

He picked up the telephone receiver. He'd just have to play it by ear; make up something as he went along.

'Graves's Garage,' he said.

'Hello, Dennis; it's Edwina Charles here. I'm sorry to trouble you, but I'm a little concerned about Alison. She arranged to call and see me this afternoon after she'd been to see Mrs Blackmore and she hasn't turned up yet. I understand from Mrs Blackmore that Alison's not very well, and I just wanted to make sure that she's all right.'

He spoke hesitantly. 'What d'you mean? She took sick or something while she was over at the church this afternoon?'

'No, Mrs Blackmore told me that Alison's father phoned cancelling her appointment at the vicarage. He said she was going to stay indoors in the warm.'

'News to me,' he said. 'Nobody's told me anything about this. As far as I'm concerned she's fine. She didn't tell me she wouldn't be seeing Mrs Blackmore this afternoon.'

'I was afraid you might say that,' confessed Mrs Charles. 'This is why I've phoned you instead of Alison's parents. I didn't want to alarm them unnecessarily, although I rather think we've no alternative now. I very much hope I'm wrong about this, Dennis, but the phone call Mrs Blackmore received this afternoon from a man claiming to be Alison's father, seems to me to have been made in very similar circumstances to a phone call I received on Wednesday morning cancelling an appointment that Judith Caldicott had made with me for the middle of the afternoon.'

There was a pause. Dennis sounded bewildered. 'I don't understand . . . What's all this got to do with Alison? Why was she going to call round and see you?'

'I can't answer that question, Dennis. As I've said, she didn't turn up, which means I haven't had an opportunity to speak with her and find out what's troubling her. And I don't really think we should waste time in discussing this matter any further for the moment, especially since there's so very little that I can tell you. The most important thing to do now is to make sure that the phone call Mrs Blackmore received today was genuine and not a hoax and that Alison is safe at home in bed.'

CHAPTER ELEVEN

'I can't help feeling that Judith Caldicott's killer has made his first real mistake, Superintendent: the phone call he made to Mrs Blackmore has to be a direct link between Alison Cockburn's disappearance and Judith's murder,' said Mrs Charles in a slow, thoughtful voice.

David Sayer had driven over to see her first thing the following morning with the latest news on the search for Alison Cockburn, who was last seen by his aunt, Margaret Sayer, as she (Alison) had walked past the old lady's cottage on her way to keep her appointment at the vicarage soon after three o'clock the previous afternoon.

Mrs Charles added, 'None of it makes any real sense to me. I simply cannot understand it; why, after all the pains he took with Judith's murder to lay the blame on my brother, he should suddenly switch the spotlight off him and turn it in an entirely different direction. It seems such a stupid thing to do. Unless we're dealing with someone who's being extremely clever in some way that we can't see.'

David looked at her. 'I don't think I follow you.'

'The phone call Mrs Blackmore received yesterday . . . So far as I can make out, everyone — including Alison's fiancé, Dennis — is of the same mind about the girl, that she's been suffering badly from pre-wedding nerves and has deliberately gone off somewhere to be on her own for a while to think things over; and that being under so much stress and strain over all the wedding preparations, and therefore overtired and incapable of thinking rationally, she tried the same ploy that everyone seems to know someone had used over Judith Caldicott's appointment with me, and simply arranged for someone — a stranger, perhaps — to phone Mrs Blackmore on her behalf and say that she was ill, to give her time to disappear before everybody, her family, started looking for her. Everyone — with what would seem to me to be the obvious, and very curious, exception of this man whom I'm inclined to think has abducted Alison — knows that she's been very upset and weepy these past few days. (So much so, in fact, that everyone has also assumed that this was why she wanted to talk to me!) Then surely it follows that if Judith's killer (this man whom I believe has now been obliged to abduct Alison because she knows something that will incriminate him in her friend's murder) — and this is assuming, of course, that he's someone we all know (someone who lives here in the village among us and who must therefore know Alison every bit as well as he knew Judith) — would've guessed what everyone would think when she went missing? Surely there was no need then of a telephone call to the vicarage cancelling her appointment? As I've said, he would've known what everyone would be likely to think when she failed to turn up on time, and he would've turned that knowledge to his advantage by *not* phoning the vicarage and running the risk of raising the alarm too soon. He's been far too clever — if he is somebody we all know — in using his knowledge of my brother and me to have made such a stupid blunder over Alison.'

'Yes, but maybe her abductor — assuming that you're right and Alison is being held somewhere against her will — had some reason for wanting to be sure that he had at least a couple of hours up his sleeve before anyone started to worry about the girl's whereabouts.'

'Perhaps . . . Though I still think I'm right, and that as I've said, the phone call was a bad mistake on his part, he needn't have made it; and that this then increases the likelihood of his being someone who knew Alison only slightly, and Judith very well (Judith herself unwittingly supplied him with information about my brother and me which he was then able to use when planning her murder). He would've had a reasonable amount of time, anyway — without the phone call to Mrs Blackmore — to carry out his plans for himself and Alison. There could've been any number of reasons why Alison was late in turning up for her appointment at the vicarage — the weather, for one. Mrs Blackmore wouldn't have got immediately on the telephone to the Cockburns or Dennis to find out what was detaining Alison. It might've been anything up to an hour or more before she thought of doing something like that; and even then, she might've decided to wait for Alison, or her parents, to contact her with either an explanation or an apology for her non-arrival. Mrs Blackburn had no reason to think there might be something wrong. And in that time, Alison's abductor could cover quite some considerable distance with her.'

'Aren't you making rather a big production out of this? I know the sudden disappearance of a young girl is something that should never be treated too lightly, but in the circumstances, I can't help feeling that you might be somewhat over-reacting to all of this.'

She shook her head. 'I don't think so. I have my own personal ideas about the cause of Alison's strange behaviour during these past few days, and I don't necessarily think it had quite so much to do with the stresses and strains of preparing for her wedding next weekend as everyone supposes.'

David looked at her hesitantly. 'Why do you think she wanted to see you?'

'I don't *think* anything, Superintendent: I know why she wanted to see me; or rather why she agreed to see me.' She smiled faintly at the quick look he shot her. 'Yes . . . I wanted to see her, not the other way round — Because of this.' She handed him the piece of notepaper that had been delivered with her newspaper the previous morning. 'Alison slipped it between the pages of my morning paper when she got the newspapers ready for the paper-boys to deliver first thing yesterday.'

He frowned as he read what was written on it. 'How did you know this was her handiwork?'

'By something her mother had told me about Alison and Judith Caldicott a couple of days earlier. It tied in with the note.'

'You should've let the police know about this.'

She gave her head a quick shake. 'I disagree. That really would've been over-reacting on my part. I wanted to be absolutely sure that I wasn't grasping at straws. Alison is in a highly emotional state, very tense and nervous about her wedding, very much on edge, and therefore prone possibly to magnifying tiny, insignificant matters out of all proportion. She was extremely distressed about Judith's death — they had once been very close friends, Tilly Cockburn has told me; and perhaps during that friendship, there'd been some bad feeling (not uncommon between teenaged girls, particularly once they start dating boys), and in her present state of mind, Alison suddenly recalled the incident and felt abnormally distressed, or guilty, about it for some reason. Both, I would think. But this was not to say that whatever had caused her to feel this way, had the slightest bearing on Judith's murder and my brother's predicament. We can all be wise after the event. At the time, I did what I thought was best . . . I went down to Mr Mortimer's shop the moment I found the note and I spoke to Alison. She refused to discuss the matter with me on the spot — Mr Mortimer was in the shop at the time and she naturally didn't want him to know anything about it — and we agreed that she should come and see me after she was through at the vicarage in the afternoon.'

'What was your impression of the girl when you spoke to her in the shop?'

'Much the same, I confess, as everyone else's. I thought she was extremely tense and nervous, and that she might possibly be blowing some minor schoolgirl squabble from the past way out of all proportion. And if I was right, then my calling in the police about the note I'd received from her was only going to add to the girl's distress and deeply embarrass her family. Quite needlessly, from my point of view.'

'What's a motor bike and Judith's uncle got to do with a schoolgirl squabble?'

'That's what I'd hoped to find out when I spoke to Alison . . . And the schoolgirl squabble is only guesswork on my part. I might be completely wrong about that and it was some other minor incident that had occurred between them in the past that upset Alison when she learned of Judith's death. As for the motor bike . . .' Mrs Charles hesitated; frowned slightly. 'Tilly told me that Judith's boy-friend — somebody, presumably, that she and Alison knew while they were at high school together in Gidding — was killed in a motor cycle accident. My impression was that the relationship between Judith and this boy was more than just the usual teenage boy/girl romance, and that up until this boy's death, Judith's sights might well have been set no higher than on getting married and settling down and raising a family. She was much like her best friend, Alison, that is. Then after this boy died, she decided to go all out for a career as a pop singer. I suspect that one of these two milestones in Judith's life saw the end of her friendship with Alison. The latter would seem the more obvious of the two; but then again, not impossibly, it was something to do with the former, the boy who died.'

David nodded musingly. 'Yes, I agree; it does sound as if there could've been a bit of jealousy between the two of them over the lad who was killed, and Alison has always felt a bit upset and guilty about it, especially when Judith too died young.'

'Exactly,' said Mrs Charles. 'There was Alison, getting married, with all the excitement of planning for the big day, her life ahead of her; and Judith, her former best friend, was dead; her life was finished. However, while I still think there's something like this behind Alison's strange behaviour over the past few days, what happened yesterday — the phone call that was made to the vicarage (by the same man, I think, who phoned me on Wednesday morning) — convinces me that there must've been more to it; something that might possibly have helped me to clear my brother. And as I've said, Judith's killer's first big mistake.'

David shook his head slowly. 'It sounds all right, but I'm not sure . . . And in any event, I don't see that it helps us much. Or your brother. If Alison does know something, then —' he shrugged '— well, I don't think you need me to spell it out for you.'

She nodded her head. 'Yes, eventually her abductor will

have to kill her. It's the only way out for him. And yet, the moment he kills her, *if* he kills her, he has in effect put the seal on his guilt over Judith's murder. And I'm assuming that in those circumstances, the police will look more closely at yesterday's phone call to the vicarage and accept that it has some direct connection with the contents of Alison's anonymous note to me. So I very much fear that the police are going to continue with their searches of the fields and woods around Little Gidding, and with their inquiries in Gidding and elsewhere, and not come up with any trace of Alison Cockburn. If she's not already dead — murdered like her friend, Judith — then she soon will be: there's no doubt in my mind about that! The police aren't searching for a missing girl who could be wandering about somewhere in the countryside suffering from amnesia brought on by pre-wedding-day stress and her added distress over the brutal murder of a former close friend: they are looking for a body; one, I suspect, that's been very well concealed.'

David thought about it for a few moments, then nodded his head. 'You put forward a very convincing argument and I've got an uncomfortable feeling that you're more than likely right. You'll never get Merton to agree with you, though. He'll take one look at that note and come up with the same theories about it that you did originally, and see it as further proof of the girl's present state of mind.' He paused; looked at the note again. 'I wonder where the uncle fits in all of this?'

'It's speculation again, of course, but he's quite a young man, not much older than Judith was; and he lives with her mother and father, was presumably living with them all the while that Judith was at high school. It occurs to me — particularly in view of the remark you made to me the other day to the effect that in your experience with this kind of murder investigation, one seldom has to look much further afield than the victim's immediate family — that her uncle might've been rather more fond of her than he should've been, and that there might've been more to the road accident in which her boy-friend was killed than met the eye. This could also tie in with her leaving home when she did for the bright lights of London. She was, in effect, getting away from home — Perhaps from the unwelcome attentions of her uncle?' she finished on a questioning note.

David spoke thoughtfully. 'I'll have to tread carefully where he's concerned, but I shouldn't have too much difficulty in checking back on the accident to see if there were any suspicious circumstances surrounding it. I'll tell you now, though, that I very much doubt that there was anything odd about it. That would've been during my stretch at Gidding, and I'd remember the incident. Motor cycle accidents are so commonplace that one involving some unusual circumstances would've stuck out like a sore thumb.'

'Then that will leave us with no alternative. In that event, we're going to have to beard the lion in its den!'

'Hopefully, it won't come to that. I tread a pretty fine line over there at Gidding, and Mike Caldicott would be just the type to raise a stink about the way Merton and some of the others turn a blind eye to my comings and goings.'

Mrs Charles looked concerned. She knew that as a security adviser to private industry, David was very much dependent on the goodwill of the police, and she was anxious not to jeopardise the particularly cordial relations he enjoyed with his friend, Detective Chief Superintendent Clive Merton, and the Gidding Constabulary as a whole. 'Please don't do anything foolish on my account,' she said. 'That's the last thing Cyril and I would want.'

He waved a dismissive hand in the air. 'Too late for warnings now: I'm well and truly hooked on this one! I'm as determined as you are to get to the bottom of this. Don't you worry, I can take care of myself — and the likes of young Caldicott, if it comes to it.'

Mrs Charles continued to look concerned. 'Perhaps we should play this a little more cautiously for the moment and look elsewhere for our answers.' She hesitated. 'What about your aunt?'

'My God,' he said. 'Alongside her, Caldicott is a positive pussy-cat! I'd sooner tackle him any day.'

'Who else did your aunt see yesterday? Besides Alison?'

'Nobody of any importance. Merton would've said something.'

'Ah,' said Mrs Charles, 'but he doesn't know what we know, does he?'

David sighed heavily. 'The things I do for you! All right, I'll have a word with the old girl myself. But I want you to know this is under sufferance. Above and beyond the call of duty!'

'I shall remember that, Superintendent,' she promised him with a solemn smile.

CHAPTER TWELVE

David thanked Mrs Pendlebury, taking the cup of coffee she handed him and then placing it on the small wine table beside him.

'Not there!' snapped his aunt. 'I've got better things to do with my time than to waste it in trying to get rid of the white rings you leave all over my furniture every time you visit me.'

'Sorry, Auntie,' he said, and dutifully picked up his cup and saucer and cradled them in his lap. 'I see you're bright and cheerful as ever.'

She glowered at him. 'Well!' she demanded. 'They found the silly girl yet?'

He glanced at Mrs Pendlebury quickly, then frowned a little at his aunt, who snorted and said, 'And you needn't look at me like that! This is exactly what we thought was going to happen, isn't it?' She narrowed her eyes challengingly at Mrs Pendlebury, who didn't reply. 'That girl's no different from the rest of them today. All they think about is clothes and their hair and that racket they call music, and getting an engagement ring on their finger.'

David glanced again at Mrs Pendlebury, who made no comment, merely raised her eyebrows a little, flicked her eyes in Miss Sayer's direction and then picked up the scarf she was knitting and carried on with it.

'You mark my words,' said Miss Sayer. 'There's some other man involved in this and she's run off with him.'

David looked quickly at Mrs Pendlebury, who discreetly indicated to him, behind his aunt's back, to take no notice, and that he wasn't to concern himself on her account.

'Wasting the taxpayers' money poking about out there in the fields,' muttered Miss Sayer. 'Asking stupid questions.'

'Like what, for instance?' asked David.

She snorted a little; said nothing for a moment. Then: 'Asking Dennis Pendlebury where *he* was when the question they should've been asking him was where was that fool Jack Graves yesterday afternoon. And on Wednesday afternoon. It's no wonder the police can't solve anything these days without appealing to the public for help with their inquiries. Thick as two planks, the lot of them. Wouldn't know what day of the week it was!'

Mrs Pendlebury shrugged her shoulders faintly and raised her eyebrows a little, as if to say, '*I've had to put up with this all morning, now it's your turn!*'

'All right, Auntie; I'll bite. Where was Jack Graves yesterday afternoon?'

The old lady pretended to have lost all interest in the conversation; concentrated her attention on the activities of one of her neighbours in his greenhouse.

'Well, Auntie; I'm waiting.'

She snorted. 'Been seeing Agnes Fisher's eldest, hasn't he? And I don't mean about that car of hers, either. On the sly; out there at Whitethatch Cottage.'

'You've no business talking like this, Miss Sayer,' said Mrs Pendlebury, putting down her knitting for a moment. She spoke crossly and looked extremely annoyed. 'Our conversation was in strictest confidence. Dennis could lose his job if it gets back to Mr Graves that I've discussed this with you.'

'*Humph!*' said Miss Sayer. 'You think I didn't already know about it? There's only one person who doesn't know about the hanky-panky that goes on over there at Whitethatch Cottage every Wednesday afternoon, and that's that half-wit Jack Graves's got for a wife.'

David looked at Mrs Pendlebury, then at his aunt. 'How long has this been going on?'

His aunt gave him a sour look; made no reply.

'Are you telling me that Graves was in Whitethatch Cottage on Wednesday afternoon with a girl?'

His aunt gave him another sour look. 'I just said so, didn't I?'

'You never said anything about seeing either one of them going past your window that afternoon.'

She looked at him as if he were mad. 'Don't talk daft! Of course they didn't go past my window. They're not that stupid! The weather's been too good, not like it was yesterday afternoon when he drove down the road in bad light, and in the pouring rain, in somebody else's car and with something deliberately stuck up on the front seat so that nobody could get a proper look at him!' She made a small pause, turning her head to look casually out of the window for a moment or two before looking back at him. 'Everybody knows he goes the other way round to Whitethatch Cottage every Wednesday so that he won't be seen.'

David stared at her in disbelief. 'You mean to say that Graves goes to all the trouble of driving out through the other side of the village, then all the way into Gidding, and then back to Whitethatch Cottage along the motorway?'

'Got to, hasn't he? — if he doesn't want people to start getting suspicious. Waste of time, of course. He and the girl were spotted over there months ago by Colonel Billingsley and his cronies while they were out walking one afternoon. That graffiti those schoolchildren have been daubing everywhere points directly at Graves and what he gets up to with some of the local girls when he's supposed to be out road-testing customers' cars. You can't keep things like that a secret from children for long. Some of them are sharp as tacks about that sort of thing. Sharper than most adults about what's going on right under everybody's nose!'

David brushed aside her remarks with an irritable wave of his hand. 'How does the girl get to the cottage?'

'She drives there, of course. She works in Gidding — serves over the counter in that chemist's shop at the top of London Road. Wednesday is her half day off, Venie Jackson was telling me the other day when she was here. Then she drives back into Gidding along the motorway, and comes home at the normal time the long way round, like he does . . . through the village.'

'How do you know they were there at the cottage together last Wednesday?'

Miss Sayer looked at Mrs Pendlebury, then she gazed out of the window again.

'Really, Miss Sayer; you've no right to talk like this,' said Mrs Pendlebury in an aggrieved voice. She rolled up her knitting and put it aside; turned to David. 'There's no way Dennis could possibly know for certain that Mr Graves was at the cottage on Wednesday afternoon with Beryl Fisher. I'm afraid your aunt is letting her imagination run away with her again. And I want you to be absolutely certain in your mind that she's come to these conclusions entirely on her own.'

Mrs Pendlebury turned and spoke scoldingly to Miss Sayer. 'You've really no business to be talking to people like this, Miss Sayer, without first making sure of your facts.'

David looked at Mrs Pendlebury. 'Your lad covers for his boss? With Mrs Graves?'

She sighed. 'He's no alternative, has he? Not that I think Dennis minds, so long as Mr Graves doesn't expect him to tell fibs for him to Mrs Graves. She's a very difficult woman, neurotic and highly-strung, and Dennis, I must admit, feels a certain sympathy for Mr Graves; but he draws the line at fibbing to Mr Graves's wife for him. She will, of course, find out the truth eventually, and I can only say I sincerely hope —' she gave Miss Sayer a stern look '— that when the truth finally does come out about her husband's little peccadilloes every Wednesday afternoon in Whitethatch Cottage and elsewhere, Dennis is not going to suffer in any way because of it.'

'What about yesterday afternoon?' David asked Mrs Pendlebury. 'My aunt just mentioned something about Graves and somebody else's car.'

'I don't know anything about that,' said Mrs Pendlebury.

'You know very well that I told you he drove past in Mr Jackson's car soon after Alison went by,' protested Miss Sayer.

'You told me about Alison, and you said, later on, that you saw Mr Jackson's car. I don't remember your mentioning anything about seeing Mr Graves.'

Miss Sayer made no comment; looked out of the window again.

'Well, Auntie?'

'Venie and Harold Jackson had tea with me on Thursday — they'd brought their car over for Graves to fix . . . that ridiculous-looking foreign one with everything all back to front that Harold Jackson insisted on buying while they were living with their daughter in Germany, and which has done nothing ever since but cost the fool every penny and more that he thought he was going to save by buying it cheap over there instead of here at home. They called in here to see how I was getting along after my fall before catching the bus back to Gidding, and Harold Jackson said Graves promised that he'd take the car back to him himself on Saturday afternoon.'

'Does he usually do that for his customers?' David asked Mrs Pendlebury in some surprise.

'I'm not sure. I wouldn't have thought so. How was he going to get back? I'd hardly think Mr Graves is the kind of man to travel by public transport.'

Miss Sayer snorted. 'That would be the day! I'll give you one guess how he got back. He was making good use of the opportunity to meet that little madam again in Whitethatch Cottage, wasn't he? Then afterwards, they drove into Gidding separately. He delivered the car to the Jacksons, left it out the front of their place and slipped the keys through the letter-box so that he wouldn't have to talk to them and risk their spotting the girl hanging about out in the road in her car waiting to give him a lift home; and then she drove him back here with her. This was at the usual time she normally finishes work of a Saturday night so nobody would wake up to what the two of them had been up to again.'

'Nobody except you, that is,' he said in a dry voice.

The old lady looked at him scornfully. 'I might look as if I'm in my dotage, but I'm not quite there just yet. You mightn't know when somebody's pulling the wool over your eyes, my boy, but Venie Jackson and I certainly do. Plain as the nose on your face what Graves's game was with their car on Saturday. All that ridiculous palaver about not troubling them, and slipping the keys through the letter-box . . . The miracle of it is that he and that girl have got away with it for so long.'

Miss Sayer narrowed her eyes; watched her nephew climb into his car and then turn it round and head towards Mrs Charles's bungalow further along the road.

'And there's somebody else who wants to stop acting so high and mighty and looking down his nose at me, and start asking himself what people must be thinking about him and the number of times he calls on that woman up the road,' she remarked at length.

'That's a dreadful thing to say, and you know it,' Mrs Pendlebury scolded her. 'You should be ashamed of yourself. Mrs Charles is a very nice person; she wouldn't dream of taking another woman's husband from her. Everybody knows they're very good friends and that they've worked together often solving those difficult murder cases that have baffled the police. And there is such a thing, you know, as plain, old-fashioned friendship.'

Miss Sayer snorted. Then, smiling slyly to herself, she remarked, 'Not getting very far with solving this one, are they?'

'Early days yet,' Mrs Pendlebury assured her. 'Though I must admit that you've made things extremely difficult for them by insisting that you didn't see Mr Forbes on Wednesday.'

Mrs Pendlebury waited expectantly, but Miss Sayer refused to rise to the bait. Craning her neck, she leaned forward in her chair and watched her nephew get out of his car, then a few moments later disappear through Mrs Charles's front door.

CHAPTER THIRTEEN

'Did you know that Jack Graves has been seeing young Beryl Fisher in that old cottage near your brother's place?' David asked Mrs Charles as they went into her sitting-room.

She shook her head.

'No, I thought not,' he said. 'I had an idea that my aunt's information might've been a relatively new piece of gossip, and confined — though not for long — to the members of the Over-Sixties' Club. And her Gidding chums, the Jacksons, of course,' he added in a wry voice. 'Still, we mustn't look a gift horse in the mouth. With any sort of luck, we could've found ourselves a couple of witnesses, somebody who saw your brother on Wednesday afternoon. Though I don't think we can expect them to be in any great rush now to come forward and do the right thing and admit publicly to where they were on Wednesday afternoon, and that they saw your brother in or near that little private lane his place shares with their love-nest. It's a delicate situation; we'll have to be very tactful about this. Graves is a fool, of course, but the girl's over age, and it's not for us to moralise about their behaviour.'

'You're quite sure the information is reliable?'

He nodded. 'Mrs Pendlebury confirmed it. Her lad's expected to cover for Graves if Mrs Graves starts asking awkward questions.'

Mrs Charles nodded; was thoughtful for a moment. 'Unfortunately, there's a very good possibility that they didn't see Cyril. You can't see his place at all from Whitethatch Cottage; so the only opportunity they would've had to see him would've been as he was cutting through the lane to the road.'

'And depending how occupied they were with one another at that precise moment — as he went past,' said David with a small smile, 'they mightn't have had the faintest idea that he was out there.'

'Let's find out, shall we?' suggested Mrs Charles.

Mrs Charles pushed open the door of the chemist's shop and went inside. Beryl Fisher was standing behind the counter. The pharmacies in Gidding worked a rota system for Sundays, and as Mrs Charles had noticed Beryl driving past her bungalow in her battered little car first thing that morning, she had assumed this to mean that it was the turn of the one at the top of London Road to open up until lunch-time to dispense any prescriptions that were needed urgently.

It was getting near to closing time and Beryl looked at her watch a trifle impatiently as Mrs Charles approached the counter. The light was at Mrs Charles's back, she was completely in shadow, and the girl didn't recognise who her late customer was until Mrs Charles was standing right before her.

Beryl was nineteen, plain to the point of being really rather ugly, and because she suffered with adenoids which caused her breathing difficulties and made it necessary for her to do most of her breathing through her mouth, which usually hung open, she tended to look a little simple-minded.

She rubbed the back of one of her hands across the tip of her noise, as if to remove a dew-drop from it, when she recognised her customer. 'Oh, hello, Mrs Charles,' she said. 'I didn't recognise you for a moment.' Her nasal condition forced her to speak through her nose which made her voice sound thick and a little choked. 'I'm very sorry, the chemist has just left. You won't be able to get a prescription made up until tomorrow morning now.' She looked pointedly at the time. 'I was just about to close.'

'Please don't let me hold you up,' said Mrs Charles. 'You go ahead and lock the door: I don't mind waiting.'

Beryl stared at her, mouth agape as usual; then she rubbed the back of her hand across the tip of her nose again and sniffed.

'You know why I'm here, don't you?' said Mrs Charles.

Beryl stared at her, and then, very slowly, colour crept up from her neck to her cheeks until they were a flaming red. 'Mr Forbes saw us, didn't he? He told you about me and Mr Graves. I told Mr Graves he would. But he said it was all right because Mr Forbes never comes out of the oast-house on Wednesday. I knew he'd see us,' she wailed. 'You're not going to tell, are you? I won't half catch it from my mum when she finds out what's been going on.'

'No, Beryl: Mr Forbes didn't see you on Wednesday afternoon; but you and Mr Graves saw him, didn't you?'

The girl stared at her. 'No,' she said. She sounded genuinely puzzled. 'Who told you that?'

'You didn't see him?'

The girl shook her head slowly.

'You're absolutely sure that neither you nor Mr Graves saw my brother walking past Whitethatch Cottage on Wednesday afternoon?'

Beryl nodded; rubbed the back of her hand back and forth across her nose. 'We talked about it . . . on Saturday afternoon. I phoned Mr Graves at the garage — he's told me I mustn't, but I simply had to, I was so upset and worried — and I told him we'd better be quick and think about what we were going to say if Mr Forbes told everybody he'd seen us. Or Mr Graves's car or mine. We always hide our cars round the back of Whitethatch Cottage where nobody can see them from the lane . . . And Mr Graves told me not to panic, it'd be all right, and then he said we'd better meet on Saturday afternoon and talk things over. I've never felt so scared in all my life: I just know my mum's going to find out, and she won't half tear a strip off me. She'll kick me out, I know she will! And then what'll I do? Mr Graves was ever so kind and got that little car for me to run to and fro in; but this is different, isn't it? He's not going to be able to help me this time, is he? What if his wife finds out? He said we'd just have to wait and see what happens, and that Mr Forbes probably wasn't telling the truth, anyway — Well, nobody really believes him, do they?' she put in defensively. 'I mean, that he came out of the oast-house on

Wednesday afternoon and went down to Roper's dairy. He was lying about that, wasn't he?' she finished on a plaintive note.

'Another dead end, I'm afraid,' Mrs Charles confessed to David half an hour later when he returned to their agreed meeting place in the London Road and picked her up. 'It was as you feared: they didn't see Cyril. They've been living in absolute dread these past few days of his having seen them. The girl felt sure that it was only a matter of time before he came up with their names as possible witnesses to his where-abouts on Wednesday afternoon. How about you? Did you fare any better with the police records?'

He shook his head regretfully. 'No luck there, either. I checked them thoroughly. Twice, in fact, in case I missed something the first time round. I can't see anything at all that would lead me to suppose there could've been more to that motor bike accident. The lad was speeding — still using learner plates, hadn't had the bike all that long — and he simply lost control of the machine going round a bend on a road.'

'No one else was involved in the accident?'

'No.'

'There must be something,' she said, a faint note of exasper-ation creeping into her voice.

'I'm sorry,' he said, and shook his head again. Then, after a small pause: 'That only leaves the uncle. We're going to have to tackle him.'

'No, that must be our very last resort. If he is involved in this in some way, we don't want to alert him to the fact that we're on to him. And in any event, he didn't strike me as being the type of person who'd go out of his way to assist us. Me, in particular. He was very hostile towards me when I called on his brother and sister-in-law.'

'And possibly for reasons other than those we originally supposed,' said David.

She nodded, and they lapsed into a thoughtful silence; didn't speak again until they turned off the motorway and onto the slip road that would take them into the village of Little Gidding.

'If there wasn't anything special, or out of the ordinary, about the motor cycle accident, what about the dead boy himself?' Mrs Charles asked at length, in a musing voice. 'Was there anything out of the ordinary or special about him?'

'Seemed a decent sort of kid,' said David. 'The chap who turned up the records for me, remembered the accident and the lad. Didn't know him personally, but his own lad knocked about with him for a time while they were altar boys over at St Anthony's.'

Mrs Charles looked at him sharply. 'At Gidding Cathedral?'

'As some people call it . . . yes,' he said, nodding. 'Why so interested?'

'What was the boy's name — Judith's friend . . . the one who was killed?'

'Barry Edmonds. That name mean something to you?'

She thought for a moment. 'No, not that I recall. But I might know somebody to whom it does mean something. That's if I can get to speak to him.'

David turned his head and looked at her. 'You're not talking about your brother, I hope?' He shook his head at her. 'Merton won't wear it. Never in a million years. No way!'

Detective Chief Superintendent Merton looked across his desk at Mrs Charles: then, with a slow shake of his head, he said, 'No way. I'm sorry to be blunt about this, but I'm very busy right now and you're wasting my time. Your brother stays right where I've got him, safely under lock and key.'

'My brother can hardly be described as being a dangerous criminal, Mr Merton,' said Mrs Charles, her tone mildly rebuking.

He looked at her coldly. 'I agree with you there. *Unco-operative* is one word that comes to mind. *Exasperating. Bloody-minded.* Oh, and *superior!* His attitude towards us has been nothing short of downright rude and arrogant. I don't think

I've ever had the misfortune to interrogate anyone with whom it is as difficult to communicate as your brother. Half the time he won't so much as condescend to acknowledge that we are even present in the room with him!'

'You misjudge him, Mr Merton. It's just that his mind is always on much higher things which means it takes a very special skill to reach him. For this reason alone, I feel you should consider very seriously my request to speak with him.' She looked Merton directly in the eye. 'If I'm not afraid to speak to him, to hear what he might have to say, why should you be? He and I are the ones who have everything to lose. You have everything to gain and nothing whatsoever to lose by my talking to him.'

'Only my sanity!' he muttered, glaring malevolently at David for having placed him in this situation.

'One must know how to put questions to Cyril to get the answers one wants,' she said after a moment. 'If, as you say, he's proving unco-operative, then I would venture to say that much of the fault lies with those interrogating him. I do not mean to be disrespectful, Mr Merton, but you are the one who's being unco-operative and bloody-minded. Please . . . I urge you most strongly to reconsider.'

He scowled at her. 'I'll need to see a list of the questions you want to ask him.'

'There's only the one important question, Mr Merton. What can he tell me about a young man named Barry Edmonds? I admit that I won't be able to put the question to him as directly as that; but this, however, will be where the things I ask him are intended to lead.'

Merton dragged his hand down the lower part of his face and tugged on his ruddy jowls. 'This is all highly irregular . . . And who is this cove, anyway — this Barry Edmonds? What's he got to do with this mess your brother's got himself into?'

'I don't know. That's what I'm hoping Cyril will be able to tell me.'

Merton tugged on his jowls again, then ran a hand over his balding scalp, sat back in his chair, gazed at Mrs Charles for a moment, then scratched his forehead irritably.

'A man must be mad!' he muttered. 'And by God, I'm warning you — both of you —' he said, fixing David with a sullen look '— that if anything goes wrong —' He broke off; scowled at Mrs Charles again. 'We're taking your brother over to his place first thing tomorrow morning to try and sort out one or two points that we're not clear on. You understand, of course, that there can be no formal arrangement between us. However, if you should chance to stop by there . . . unexpectedly, as it were — say, at somewhere around eleven o'clock — and you should manage to say a few words to your brother in the process, there isn't a lot anybody can do about it, is there? If you follow my meaning.'

'Very clearly, thank you, Mr Merton.'

The Chief Superintendent looked suddenly at David. 'You two aren't holding out on me about something again, are you?'

David shook his head. 'I only wish we were, Clive,' he said.

Mrs Charles rose. 'Forgive me, but would I be speaking out of turn if I were to ask if there's any news yet of Alison Cockburn's whereabouts?'

'Nothing definite, but we're following a lead that came in a short while ago that looks promising. A girl answering to her description was spotted boarding a late train for London last night.'

Merton paused; looked from one to the other of them. 'Well?' he snapped. 'No dramatic pronouncements? Not from either one of you? My God, don't tell me I'm actually doing something right for a change? I don't believe it!'

Mrs Charles and David exchanged glances; made no comment.

CHAPTER FOURTEEN

David got up from the sofa and went and stood at the window looking out at the road. His wife, Jean, smiled apologetically at Mrs Charles and said, 'He's been like that ever since he got home last night; can't sit still for a minute.'

Jean, a pretty, slim woman in her fifties, had accompanied her husband to the village to lend him — as he had put it — *'a little moral support'*, when he paid his duty call on his Aunt Margaret that morning.

Mrs Charles said, 'I've been much the same myself.' The smile on her lips faded. 'I don't like to admit it, but I very much suspect that Cyril's our last hope. I've thought about it all night, and I don't honestly see that there's much more we can do if my talk with him this morning finishes in the same dead end that everything else we've tried seems to.'

Jean looked concerned; turned to her husband. 'Perhaps that's because of Mr Forbes's —' She looked back quickly at Mrs Charles. 'I mean, because he's your brother,' she explained. 'It's very difficult to see things clearly when one has such a big personal vested interest in a particular outcome. I know it wouldn't be an easy thing to do, but have you tried looking at everything the other way round and tackling the problem from that angle? Just for argument's sake, of course.' She hesitated. 'I'm not suggesting for one moment that Mr Forbes isn't telling the truth about what he did on Wednesday afternoon. But what if —? Well, forgive me for saying so —' She blushed under the faintly disapproving glance her husband shot at her, then tossed her head slightly in defiance as she continued, '— Mr Forbes is a little vague, I understand. What if he made a mistake about which way he went when he left his place to go down to the dairy? Maybe he didn't walk along the road; maybe he went some other way, and that's why David's aunt didn't see him.'

Mrs Charles nodded. 'I've wondered about that myself,' she admitted.

David turned his head from the window to look at her. 'And?' he prompted when she fell silent.

She spoke musingly. 'What if he's telling the truth and your aunt is also telling the truth? Cyril did walk along the road, and Miss Sayer didn't see him.'

'That's not possible,' said David.

'Agreed,' she said. 'But if we accept that both are telling the truth, then where is the lie that proves it. There has to be one buried somewhere deep within the two truths where we can't see it. Perhaps, for example, as Cyril approached your aunt's cottage that afternoon, and realising that she'd probably be sitting in her window as usual, he took some evasive action that he's since completely forgotten all about. I know it's not going to help our case in any way, but at least it would explain why both are apparently so obdurate on this point.'

'And that says it all,' said David. 'Neither will budge an inch. My aunt certainly won't.'

Mrs Charles agreed. 'The mere fact that Cyril's been prepared to commit himself to such a positive statement testifies to that. And yet it's strange . . . It's bothered me all along. I can't help feeling that because neither will give in to the other and admit that a mistake's been made, this is where our attention should be focused; and whereas previously we've assumed that one of them is lying, we should, perhaps, accept that both are telling the truth and work from there.'

'But,' said Jean, 'as David pointed out, they can't both be telling the truth: it simply isn't possible.'

Mrs Charles nodded her head thoughtfully; sighed. 'Where are we going wrong? What are we missing? There's something we haven't seen, I'm sure of it.'

David turned from the window and said, 'Right, let's go back over everything from the beginning and see what we've got. We'll start with the victim herself, Judith Caldicott.'

'Why was she consulting you?' Jean asked Mrs Charles.

Then, glancing at her husband, and with an apologetic grimace: 'Oh, I'm sorry: I'm not supposed to ask those sorts of questions, am I? I forgot.'

'No, it's quite all right,' said Mrs Charles. 'We must examine everything if we're to get at the truth. I don't feel that it's necessary for me to go into too many details: suffice it to say that Judith wanted to quit the entertainment scene — she couldn't cope with it, the pressures that come with that sort of life. At the same time, however, she was very unsure about whether she'd be doing the wise thing by giving it all up now, while she was right at the very top of her profession. She knew that she was in a very fickle industry, and that her chances of getting back to the kind of position she was in at that moment, were probably slim. This was if, at some later stage, she had a change of heart and wanted to pick up where she had left off. It was a very difficult decision for her to make.'

David said, 'Are you absolutely sure that this was the real problem; that it wasn't something nearer to home — a family matter, something to do with her uncle, say, and our suspicions that he might've been a little too fond of her?'

Mrs Charles considered the question, then shook her head. 'No. I could be wrong of course, but so far as I was concerned, her emotional problems were directly related to her career as a pop-rock singer. And this, I feel, is borne out by the trouble she was having with her throat, which I would say was largely psychosomatic and would've gradually cleared up and disappeared altogether once she'd made her decision to break away completely from the pop scene.'

'I wonder where this chap she was living with figures in all of this — these future plans of hers?' said David. 'That's something we could be overlooking. Remember what young Stanton said the other day — that groups like Ben Shipwell's are two a penny and that the group was nothing without her.'

'Yes,' said Mrs Charles. She paused; thought for a moment. 'I have rather tended to overlook him.'

'It's not too late,' Jean piped up. 'John's going down to London to see Ben Shipwell after lunch today. I'm sure he'll be only too pleased to help you in any way he can. He's got an appointment with him late this afternoon. The *'Sketch'* is sending him down to get Ben Shipwell's side of the story — the one the Caldicotts' next-door neighbour gave them — before they decide whether or not they're going to print it.'

'My God,' said David, 'I hope Shipwell and Judith Caldicott haven't sunk any of their money into valuable *objet d'art*; or if they have, it's all securely nailed to the floor!' He looked at Mrs Charles. 'Well, what do you say? Shall I get in touch with young John and see what I can fix up?'

She nodded. 'I'd like to go with him, if it could be arranged. There are several questions I'd like John to ask Ben Shipwell on my behalf, and I'd like to be there to watch his reaction to them.'

'But if Ben Shipwell knows who you are, that Mr Forbes is your brother,' said Jean 'won't that make him a bit hostile towards you and clam up?'

'I'll just have to be devious about who I really am, won't I?' said Mrs Charles, and David smiled to himself. No one could be more devious than Edwina Charles, a.k.a. Madame Adele Herrmann, when she set her mind to it. This was one of the first discoveries he had made about her.

She indicated to him to go ahead and use the telephone and he picked up the receiver and dialled the number of the local newspaper; asked to speak to John Stanton.

'All fixed,' he said as he rang off a few minutes later. 'John'll be here to collect you at two o'clock, if that's all right with you. Oh, and by the way, you're his aunt. He'll tell Shipwell that he brought you down to London with him to do some shopping.'

Mrs Charles smiled. 'That'll do nicely, thank you,' she said.

Jean looked at her. 'Did Judith mention Ben Shipwell to you?' she asked.

'No, not specifically.' Mrs Charles fell silent; reflected for a moment on the prophecy of the Tarot for Judith, the sinister warning of *The Moon* card. Then she said, 'Like most people when they become severely emotionally distressed, Judith was completely self-absorbed, unable to see beyond her own personal immediate needs and wants, and as so often is the case, this blinkered view of life was her downfall.'

It was getting near to the time that Mrs Charles would have to leave her home and walk along the road to her brother's house to meet and talk with him as arranged with Merton the previous afternoon, and Jean was watching the clock anxiously. It was not often that she found herself with an opportunity to share in one of David and Mrs Charles's investigations, and she was determined to make the most of the moment.

'What about Judith's people?' she asked. 'What are they like?'

'Rather disagreeable, I regret to have to say,' replied Mrs Charles. 'However, they don't appear to have loomed very large in Judith's life. Not latterly. In fact, I don't recall her once referring to them directly. Judith was basically very much her own woman.'

'They weren't pressuring her to stay in show business?' asked Jean.

'If they were, then she was neither allowing it to distress her nor to influence her in any way,' said Mrs Charles. 'As I've said, Judith was solely concerned with Judith; how she felt about things, what she wanted. Judith came first and last. Which isn't to say that she was a selfish girl. In her frame of mind, it was quite impossible for her to focus on anybody but herself and her own immediate needs.'

'What about this peeping Tom young Stanton told us about?' said David. 'Could she have known, or thought, that someone was spying on her and been secretly worried about it?'

'Perhaps. But she certainly never mentioned anything of that nature to me. Had I read the Tarot again for her on the afternoon of the day she died, I might have detected a definite shift in her attitude since the previous week's reading, and that there was some worry over and above her concern about her career as a singer that was suddenly preying on her mind. But this wasn't to be.'

David said, 'This attack of the vapours young Alison Cockburn succumbed to before she upped and went missing

. . . You don't think there's any chance that they were both upset about the same thing — something to do with this lad who was killed?'

Mrs Charles shook her head slowly. 'I very much doubt it. Right up to, and including, the last reading I did for her, Judith was only upset about herself. I never once heard her speak at any length, and other than in passing, of anybody but herself. And taking into account the period of time that she'd been seeing me, I know from experience that if something or someone else were troubling her, sooner or later she would've given me some indication of it. My readings of the Tarot for her persistently foretold of some kind of danger lurking constantly in the background, the kind of danger which is there to be seen if one is vigilant and keeps a careful watch, but which always ultimately succeeds in catching one unawares. Put simply, the threat to Judith's life was there — it had been there, I believe, for a very long time and stemmed from an unpleasant incident which occurred many years ago — but her total self-absorption, both recently and in the past, prevented her from seeing it. We cannot hope to get to the bottom of her murder until we know more of her past, the people who shared a hand in forming it, and in particular, if any noteworthy occurrence took place during those years — something, perhaps, that without her realising it, altered the entire course of her life.'

'Is this our mistake?' asked David. 'Are we trying too hard to connect people and incidents that are totally unrelated —? A sex pervert who skulks about at the bottom of the garden late at night hoping for a free peep-show. An uncle who might've been too fond of his niece, and who may or may not have some information concerning a road accident that could prove to be pertinent to our inquiries. The murder victim's inability — or unwillingness — to cope with the career she'd carved out for herself. A neighbour who was squabbling with Judith's family about a stolen black lace brassiere which finally turns up knotted tightly round the dead girl's throat. An argument between Judith and her lover early in the morning of the day she was murdered. A motor cycle accident some years ago in which a young man died. A young girl — one who is about to be wed — who is suddenly forced, by circumstances, to remember that accident, and feels, perhaps, guilty about it for some reason, and who has since gone missing. A middle-aged man and a young nineteen-year-old girl who meet clandestinely once a week in an old empty cottage that stands practically on the front door-step of the house in which Judith was murdered —'

'And the Punch and Judy man,' Mrs Charles finished for him in a quiet voice, 'who runs like a thread stitching them all together.'

'Not the sex pervert, surely?' Jean protested, flushing a bright scarlet when neither Mrs Charles nor David responded.

CHAPTER FIFTEEN

Mrs Charles gave her brother an exasperated look. 'You really must try and think, Cyril.'

'It's important, is it?'

'Yes, Cyril. Very important.'

'Oh,' he said, and immediately lapsed into a brooding silence. He was a small man with Mediterranean colouring, dark hair and eyes, and having a large, hooked nose, bore an uncanny likeness to the character, *Mr Punch*, in the puppet play with which he once used to entertain children. He was some years younger than his tall, fair-haired and blue-eyed sister (*half*-sister since they shared the same mother but had different fathers), and unless told, no one would suspect for one moment that they were so closely related.

At length, Mrs Charles said, 'Well, Cyril?'

'Never heard of him before in my life.'

'But you must have. If he was an altar boy, then the chances are that he was also in the choir at some time.'

Cyril looked at her vaguely. 'What was his name again?'

'Edmonds, Barry Edmonds.'

He thought for a moment. 'Might've been the boy with the voice of a bullfrog. Stuck him up the back in the finish and told him to shut up and mime if he was going to insist on staying in the choir.' He frowned at his sister. 'Can't remember. You know I haven't got your memory. I can never remember names.'

'Barry Edmonds owned a motor cycle.'

Cyril's dark eyes showed a glimmer of interest. 'What sort?'

'I forgot to ask.'

'Oh,' he said, and lapsed back into another brooding silence.

Merton, who was standing with his back to the window listening to all of this, exchanged thoughtful glances with the young police constable standing beside the door.

Mrs Charles realised that she had made a bad mistake in not getting the make of the motor cycle concerned. She had been so intent on stressing to Merton the importance of the way in which questions were phrased before they were put to Cyril, that she had completely overlooked the fact that as often as not, it could be the answers one gave him to the questions he asked that ultimately triggered off his memory and got it working along the right lines. She tried again. 'Think about it, Cyril . . . A boy who served on the altar, who maybe used to sing in the choir — like a bullfrog, if you insist. A boy-friend of Judith Caldicott's, who owned a motor cycle on which he was killed.'

There was a long silence. Then Cyril said, 'His voice broke later than usual. Couldn't sing anyway, not even before it broke. Don't know why he insisted on being in the choir. The fifty pence, I suppose.'

'I'm not following you, Cyril.'

He spoke impatiently. 'For singing at weddings. That's what they got, the choristers. At least I think it was fifty pence. I can't remember now. Maybe it was only twenty-five pence. It was a shilling when I was a lad. I remember that.'

He looked at his sister hopefully.

She sighed and rose; turned to Merton, who grinned crookedly at her and said, 'Well, Madame . . . Satisfied?'

'Yes, I think so, thank you.'

He looked smug; sniggered: couldn't resist it. 'Learn anything to your advantage?'

She looked at him for a moment, then at her brother. 'Very probably,' she replied.

'You amaze me,' he said in a dry voice.

'Yes,' she said thoughtfully, still looking at her brother. 'I must go now, Cyril. Promise me you'll think about the things we've discussed.'

He nodded, a vacant look in his eye.

She looked at him for a moment longer, then nodded to

Merton and went with him to the door.

'*Del* . . .'

Mrs Charles paused in the doorway and looked back at her brother, one of the few people who used the diminutive of her real given name, Adele. 'Yes, Cyril.'

His brows knit closely together. 'You be careful. There's a maniac loose out there. He'll be watching you.'

'Yes, I know that, Cyril. I'll be careful.'

Merton looked at them both. Something about the clairvoyant's voice, the look in her brother's eye, made him feel uneasy. Anyone else and Merton would have said Mrs Charles's response was simply intended to humour her brother. But looking at the two of them, as he was now, he knew they were both in deadly earnest. *Or equally barmy*, he thought irritably.

Mrs Charles looked at her watch; decided she had enough time to walk into the village and call in at the Post Office Stores to see Tilly Cockburn before John Stanton called to collect her at two o'clock for their trip down to London.

Mrs Charles found Tilly, at length, at home. Tilly had taken the day off and was waiting anxiously by the telephone for some news of her missing daughter.

'I can't think what on earth has got into the girl,' she said. She turned her head from her visitor and gazed wistfully at the telephone, as if willing it to ring. 'She's never done anything like this before.'

'Alison gave no indication that she might've been thinking of running off?' inquired Mrs Charles.

'I knew,' said Richard Cockburn, coming suddenly into the room. He had complained of a worsening sore throat and had been excused from attending school that day.

'You knew nothing of the sort,' said his mother. 'Go back upstairs to bed and keep warm. I'll be up with some lunch in a little while.'

'I'm hungry now,' he said.

'Well, go into the kitchen and get some bread and jam. I'm busy right now.'

'What makes you think your sister might've been planning on running away?' Mrs Charles asked the boy.

'Don't encourage him,' said Tilly. She spoke good-naturedly and managed a wan smile. 'He makes everything up as he goes along. We are becoming very worried about you, aren't we, Richard?' she added, giving her son a meaningful look.

'Alison's got a secret lover, that's how I know,' he said.

'That will do, Richard,' said his mother. 'Now, run along out to the kitchen and get something to eat.'

'It's true,' he protested. 'She was writing a mushy letter to him. I saw her! You ask her when she gets back. She'll tell you. She was upstairs bawling her eyes out, and I saw her. She wouldn't let me see it, and then she hid it in the top drawer of her dressing-table. I bet I know who it was to. She's in love with him and he's in love with her. I saw him kissing her.'

'That's quite enough, Richard,' said Tilly. She hesitated; looked at him crossly. 'You haven't been going through all the drawers in Alison's room by any chance, have you — looking for this letter that I haven't any doubt doesn't exist? You wait until your father gets home! I spent ages tidying up in there. Those drawers were turned upside-down when I went up there this morning.'

'I never touched them!' he exclaimed. 'Do me a favour! I wouldn't be seen dead in her mouldy old room. *Yuk!*'

He grimaced and groaned, then turned to go and get his bread and jam.

Mrs Charles called him back. 'Who did you see kissing your sister, Richard?'

He glanced at his mother, then looked at Mrs Charles. 'I can't tell you. Mum'll kill me. But I'm not fibbing,' he added, flashing his mother a defiant look. 'He kisses all the girls.' The boy grimaced again; made a few yukking noises. 'Everybody knows that, except her . . . Mum. He's always chasing after the girls and chatting them up. That's why Alison was bawling her head off all the time. Because she's madly in love with Mr Graves and she doesn't want to get hitched to boring old Dennis.' The boy looked wide-eyed at his mother; backed away from her. 'It's true; I swear it! Cross my heart and hope to die! You ask her if she didn't get Mr Graves to phone Mrs Blackmore for her and say she wasn't coming —'

The boy didn't like the threatening way his mother was looking at him, and so he turned with a sudden yelp and vanished in the direction of the kitchen.

'I don't know what we're going to do with that boy,' said Tilly with an exasperated sigh. 'The things he comes out with! You can't believe a word he says.'

Mrs Charles made no comment. She changed the subject. 'You've heard nothing at all from Alison since she left?'

'Not a word.'

'What about this young girl who was reported as having been seen boarding a train for London on Saturday night? Were the police able to trace her?'

'Yes. She fitted Alison's description perfectly, but unfortunately it turned out it wasn't her.' Tilly sighed. 'I don't know . . . You think you know your children, and then something like this happens and you realise that, really, in many respects they're complete strangers to you.'

'Yes,' agreed Mrs Charles. 'No matter how close we are to someone, we never know exactly what's in the other person's mind, even though we might like to think we do. They can always surprise us.'

'She's done that all right. I simply cannot understand it . . . why — if something was bothering her and making her unhappy — she didn't come to me and talk things over. She always used to.'

'Could it have been something she was afraid to tell you, do you think? Something concerning Judith Caldicott?'

Tilly looked surprised. 'Judith?' She hesitated. 'I don't think so. Admittedly, she was very upset about her . . .' Her voice tailed off into a puzzled silence.

'You said you and Judith's family — her parents, that is — have never met, didn't you? What about her uncle? I met him the other day when I called on the Caldicotts to offer them my condolences, and I was rather surprised to find that he was such a young man, not much older than Judith, I shouldn't have thought.'

Tilly shook her head. 'No, I've never met him, either. Alison didn't seem to like him much, for some reason or other. That time I was telling you about — when Judith wanted Alison to spend the weekend with her and her family, and Alison didn't want to go . . . It was because of him. I don't really know why, she wouldn't tell me: she just said Judith's uncle would be there, and that he made her feel uncomfortable, and she'd rather not go. She didn't mind going there during the day with Judith — I mean, if he was about the place — but the idea of staying overnight with the Caldicotts didn't seem to appeal to her at all. Alison was like that, though. She was a great one for her home. Wanted to go out and have fun, but at the end of the day, she liked to know that she was coming back here to her own home. I was the same at her age. Shy, more than anything — though you wouldn't think it to look at me now,' she finished with a smile.

'Did Alison ever make any comment to you about Judith's uncle in relation to that motor cycle accident you mentioned to me the other day?'

Tilly looked surprised. 'No, I don't think so. Why do you ask?'

Mrs Charles looked at her for a moment. Then she said, in a thoughtful voice, 'Do you think Alison might've been brooding about that accident for some reason or other?'

Tilly stared at her. 'But that happened years ago!'

'Yes, I know. But perhaps Judith's death suddenly reminded Alison of the accident and it upset her all over again.'

'I honestly don't know,' confessed Tilly. 'That thought never occurred to me. It was all so long ago.'

'Can you remember any details of the accident?'

'No, I'm afraid not. I didn't know the boy at all. He wasn't anyone from around here. He lived in Gidding, I think . . . I'm not even sure of that.'

'Would you happen to know if he was a chorister at St Anthony's?'

'Judith was, I know that.' Tilly hesitated. 'Yes, I believe he was. I think I can remember Alison saying — this was after he'd been killed — that some years earlier, her whole class went along to the cathedral once to hear him sing at a special service. He was a boy soprano — until his voice broke . . . I don't know what happened then, whether he still had a nice voice and could sing or not.'

'Was Alison ever a member of the choir?'

'No.' Tilly shook her head. 'She talked about it once or twice, but nothing ever came of it. It was never really on. It was much too far for her to go for choir practice; and it wasn't as though she had any sort of singing voice. It always sounds rather flat to me.' Tilly looked at Mrs Charles and a strange expression crossed her face. 'Something's wrong, isn't it? She is coming home, isn't she? You don't think something terrible has happened to her?'

'I hope not, Tilly,' said Mrs Charles in a grave voice.

Tilly looked at her hesitantly. 'Why did Alison want to see you?'

'I've no idea, Tilly. I only wish I did know. It could help us to find her.'

Tilly stared at her. 'Alison's dead, isn't she?' Her voice rose in a shrill wail. '*I knew she was; I've said it all along. My Alison is dead!*'

CHAPTER SIXTEEN

M̲rs Charles was not particularly impressed with Ben Shipwell. He was not a likeable young man. He had not bothered to shave (John Stanton told her later that he had never seen Shipwell other than with facial growth that varied in length from a few days' stubble to a wildly unkempt beard): his long, dark brown hair was greasy and secured at the back of his head in a rubber band; and there was some considerable doubt in Mrs Charles's mind as to whether he had bathed his person, or washed any of the designer rags he was wearing, in the recent past. He was aggressive, egotistical, self-centred and if he had been truly in love with Judith, which Mrs Charles seriously doubted, was bearing up remarkably well over his loss. The only expressions of grief that he made in her presence were reserved solely for the loss of his easy meal-ticket, to which — in one way or another, regardless of what he and his interviewer, John Stanton, were discussing — he inevitably returned.

Shipwell did not co-own the London home which Judith and he had shared — an ugly Gothic mansion in Kensington: the Caldicotts, however, had (according to him) a cat in hell's chance of getting him out without a fight in the law courts. (Evicting him and the tribe of hangers-on who seemed to Mrs Charles to fill every nook and cranny of the mansion, was apparently high on the list of the Caldicotts' priorities in sorting out their late daughter's financial affairs.)

The huge room in which the interview was being given was furnished in the style of a nomadic Arab tribesman — no chairs at all, just large, lumpy, garishly-coloured, satin-covered cushions that had been casually scattered about here and there. There were no wall decorations of any description, which moved Mrs Charles to consider the possibility that the young man had stripped the room of all its valuables (including its furniture) before the Caldicotts or their legal representatives moved in on him wanting to make an inventory of the contents of the mansion.

'You used to do a bit of singing yourself, though, when you first formed your group,' remarked John Stanton finally, as pre-arranged with Mrs Charles, and with a casual adroitness that was completely at odds with his physical gaucheness.

Shipwell nodded. He spoke morosely. 'Nothing to say I wouldn't have made it to the top, either.'

'I remember hearing you sing one of your own songs once,' said John. 'You were good.'

Shipwell shrugged; looked even more morose.

'There have been that many different versions of how you and Judith Caldicott originally teamed up with one another — probably none of them true,' said John with an engaging smile, 'and I've often wondered how you two really got together. I know that you were both choristers at St Anthony's, but how did you —?'

Shipwell interrupted. 'What's this St Anthony's?'

'Gidding Cathedral.'

'Didn't know they had one.'

'They haven't, not strictly speaking. That's just what the local people call it. Are you saying that this wasn't where you and Judith first met?'

Shipwell shook his head. 'Never been inside a church in my life. I'm not religious. Wouldn't have said Judith was, either; although she put on a bit of a show for that smarmy creep Sharda she was letting mess with her mind. It's all a load of bunk. No, Judith and I met at a club down here in London where I was singing with my group. I'd never been to Gidding — never heard of the place when she told me that was where she was from. Which doesn't surprise me, having finally seen the dump. That place has to be the pits! No wonder Judith got out.'

John gave him another engaging smile. 'Oh, I don't know . . . It's not so bad once you get to know the place properly.'

'I don't intend to. One look was enough for me.'

'You've only been there the once?' asked John. 'When you went up to see Judith last Wednesday?'

Shipwell shrugged; said nothing.

'You're not denying that you drove up to Gidding to see her on Wednesday?'

'The nosy old cow next door said she saw me, didn't she?'

'Yes, but . . .'

'Then I must've been there, mustn't I?'

'You've no objections to our printing the story?'

'Glad of the publicity!'

'Would you care to tell me what took place between you and Judith when you went to see her?'

'Sure. Why not?' Shipwell looked at John steadily for a moment. Then he dipped into his shirt-pocket for a packet of cigarettes and lit one up. 'I wanted to know when she was coming back to London and exactly where I stood. We argued, kissed and made up, then argued some more, and that was it. I had a meeting down here in the afternoon with the members of my group, so I said ta-ta to her and drove straight back.'

'Did she tell you what her plans were?'

Shipwell shrugged. 'She reckoned she still hadn't got her head together.'

'What do you mean by that?'

'Exactly that. She couldn't make up her mind what she wanted. I don't think she would've ever known what she wanted. That's the penalty you pay for sitting about moping and thinking too much instead of getting up and getting on with it.'

'Did Judith mention anything to you while you were with her on Wednesday about the fight she and her family were having with their next-door neighbours over her brassiere — the one that was allegedly stolen from off the washing-line and then finished up tied round her neck by whoever killed her?'

Shipwell stared at him. 'You must be joking!'

'What about the prowler that had been seen hanging around at the bottom of the Caldicotts' back garden at night?'

'Takes all types!'

'Yes, but did she say anything to you about him? Was it worrying her? I noticed the T.V. camera over your front door when we arrived, so you're reasonably security conscious. And Judith wasn't called a sex goddess for nothing. I've read about the bodyguard who used to accompany her down here everywhere she went, and it seems odd to me that she wasn't more nervous about travelling round and about Gidding so freely, even if it was her home town.'

'She said her uncle would look out for her. The one who's a copper.'

'Yes, but he couldn't be with her twenty-four hours a day the way her usual minder was. And he's only an ordinary bobby — nobody with any special pull who could arrange for her to get the kind of protection one usually associates with someone in her position.'

Shipwell shrugged. 'It was her decision. She'd been in the business long enough to know the risks she was taking.'

'Didn't it bother you?'

'Not especially. If that was the way the silly bitch wanted it, then that was her funeral.'

Shipwell didn't flinch at the crassness of his remark; wasn't even aware of its unfortunate connotations. He went on, 'It was a mystery to me where this sudden burst of filial love and affection of hers came from. They all fought like cat and dog; hated one another's guts. Her parents never came anywhere near her; didn't want to know until her name started cropping up everywhere and she really started coining it in. She told them to get lost when they tried to butt in and tell her what to do. A day was about as much as she could take of any of them.'

'How much do you think the death of her old boy-friend might've had to do with influencing her decision to go home and sort out her life?'

'What boy-friend is this?'

'The one who was killed in Gidding on a motor bike. You knew about him, didn't you?'

'She never mentioned anything about this to me. Don't tell me this was what was really bugging her! Who was this guy?'

'That's funny . . .' John paused deliberately. 'I must've got hold of the wrong end of the stick. I thought you all knew one another. He used to sing in St Anthony's choir . . . But as you've said, that wasn't where you and Judith met. His name was Barry Edmonds. He used to be a boy soprano.'

'Ducky,' said Shipwell with a faint sneer.

'Did Judith talk to you much about him?'

'This is the first I've heard of him. There were a couple of guys down here that she used to knock about with before I came on the scene, and as far as I knew, there wasn't anyone else. Nobody she was likely to lose any sleep over, that is. How did she find out about this guy? When she left here to go home, she told me she hadn't heard from her parents in months. She was just going to walk in on them, and if they slammed the door in her face, that was it, too bad, nothing she could do about it!'

John glanced at Mrs Charles. Then he said, 'I don't know who told her about Edmonds. A friend, probably.'

'Didn't know she had any of them, either,' said Shipwell. 'Not back home. She told me that when she left there to come down here and try to make a go of it as a pop-rock singer, she shook the dust of that place — Gidding — and everyone in it, off her feet forever.'

'Well, what did you make of him?' asked David when he telephoned Mrs Charles that evening to find out how she and John Stanton had fared over John's interview with Shipwell. 'Can we cross him off our list?'

'I think so,' she replied. 'He would, I think, be capable of violence if he were pushed too hard, but he had far too much to lose by Judith's death.'

'But she was going to leave him, anyway,' David pointed out. 'Things were shaping up that way, weren't they? Maybe, in those circumstances, there was something to be gained by killing her.'

'I must admit that the mansion they shared tended to look as if it had been stripped of its possessions. And the chances are that some of Judith's money, at least, would've been used for the acquisition of valuable paintings . . . investments of that nature which would more than likely have been kept housed in her home, and which means, of course, that they were readily removable. However, he has what would appear to be a cast-iron alibi for the afternoon of the murder — a business appointment he kept in London. The mere fact that he mentioned it — and my feeling was that he did so deliberately — indicates to me that he knows he's got nothing to worry about if anybody suddenly decides to start checking up on his whereabouts that afternoon.'

'Could he tell you anything about Barry Edmonds?'

'No. He claimed he didn't know him, and I think we can believe him. He assumed — I thought quite genuinely — that the boy's death was recent and that it was a contributory factor to Judith's decision to return home when she did. He didn't appear to know that it was actually the Indian holy man she was consulting in London, Sharda, who gave her this piece of advice.'

'What about this Indian guy? Is he anyone you know?'

'No, not personally. I had hoped to call on him while John and I were in London, but the person I spoke to over the telephone beforehand (and you'll forgive my suspicious nature, but I very much suspect that it was Sharda himself!), told me that Sharda returned home to India on a visit to see his own family first thing last Wednesday morning — a good six hours or more, it was stressed to me, before Judith Caldicott was murdered,' she said with a small smile. 'My impression was that we won't hear or see anything of Sharda again until this whole business is cleared up.'

'So that's that. Back to square one again!'

'I'm afraid so.'

'How did young Stanton make out? Any accidents?'

'No, he conducted himself with remarkable aplomb,' said Mrs Charles with a laugh. 'How was your visit to your aunt? Is she still making good progress?'

'As far as her thigh is concerned, yes . . . that seems fine. Jean thought she could see a marked deterioration in the old lady in other respects, though. It's been a while since Jean's been able to make a visit over there — the two of them don't really get along all that well — and she says Aunt Margaret's got a lot more rigid and finicky about things. You know how cranky and irritable some elderly folk can become about trivial little things as they grow older . . . They don't like to see you diving into the butter with your knife — you've got to scrape the knife gently over it so you don't destroy its nice, neat shape; and you must remember never to irritate her by offering her more than one cup of tea . . . and that's got to be served exactly how she likes it, not too full because her hand shakes a bit now while she's holding her cup! And so on and so forth. She's a bit of a trial, I must admit, but I'm used to her; I take no notice of it all. '*Water off a duck's back!*' — as she says to me when she's scolding me about something I've done to irritate her. Still, she's part of life's rich fabric. I'd miss not having her around.'

'Yes, I know how you feel,' she said in a thoughtful voice. 'I feel very much the same about Cyril.'

There was a small pause. Then David said, hesitantly, 'I've heard from Merton. I take it your talk with your brother wasn't the resounding success we'd hoped for.'

'No. My fault. I should've known that something as inconsequential — to us, that is — as the make of a motor cycle would be of paramount importance to Cyril, and that without it, his thinking processes would seize up completely. I should've asked . . . I don't suppose, while you were going through the records of the accident, you happened to notice the make of the bike that Barry Edmonds was riding when he was killed?'

'Yes, I did, as a matter of fact. It was a *Norton.*'

'Could you ask Mr Merton to give Cyril that piece of information for me, please?'

'Well, I could, but I'd rather not. It's not likely to get us anywhere, is it?'

'With Cyril, Superintendent, one never knows!'

CHAPTER SEVENTEEN

This sort of thing was maddening; it really got on her nerves. That travelling-rug had been folded up on the foot of the bed in the spare room for months, and now, the moment she needed it for something, it was nowhere to be found.

Sylvia Graves marched from room to room, growing more angry and frustrated by the minute, then finally thundered downstairs and went through to the butcher's shop where her father-in-law, Sam, oblivious of his raw meat-contaminated hands, was ravenously devouring a thick, corned beef sandwich in between the loud gulps he was taking from a mug of steaming hot tea.

'I'm still eating my lunch,' he said, putting down his sandwich on the bloodied chopping block, and then brushing the breadcrumbs from his mouth with the back of his large, hairy hand. 'I'll give you a shout when I'm finished.'

His daughter-in-law looked at him impatiently. She was a tall, thin, humourless woman with bright blue eyes that were stark and staring under a permanently fixed frown. Sam Graves couldn't remember the last time he'd heard Sylvia laugh or seen her smile. He didn't like her much; never had; had warned his son that he was making a mistake in marrying her, that she'd be frigid, cold as frogs' knees.

'Have you touched that travelling-rug I left folded up in the spare room?' she demanded. 'I'm going to need it to replace the one I've taken off Jack's bed and put in the washing-machine.'

Sam Graves was a slow thinker, and an even slower talker; the more so — deliberately, as she suspected — when his shrewish daughter-in-law was in one of her autocratic moods and snapping round everybody's heels to bring them into line.

'The one with the brown checks?' he said after due consideration of her question.

'We don't have another one, do we? I can't remember seeing another one, not while I've been living under this roof. It's always the same. The moment I want something, it disappears. As if I haven't got enough to do this morning. This is going to put me all behind with everything. You'll be lucky if you see dinner much before eight o'clock tonight, if then.'

'There was a black and green one once somewhere about the place, I seem to recall,' drawled Sam Graves in a thoughtful voice. 'Wonder what became of that?' He picked up the last of his sandwich and chewed pensively on it.

'It's the brown one I want.'

He drank some of his tea, then carefully replaced the mug on the chopping block; wiped the back of his hand across his mouth. 'That husband of yours had one tucked under his arm a few weeks back. Don't know that it was the brown one, though. Can't remember. He took it through to the garage, as I remember it.'

'What for?'

'I didn't think to ask him. Maybe he was taking one of his girl-friends out for a picnic and a bit of slap and tickle that afternoon. It can get very damp out there in the fields on all that grass.' Sam Graves knew that his son had an eye for the ladies, and that he'd had a number of affairs with local women over the years: the old man was quite confident, however, that his daughter-in-law knew nothing of this philandering on the part of her husband, and he felt perfectly safe in making a joke of something which he knew was, in all probability, the absolute truth.

She turned to go, hesitated; looked at him. The dirty old devil often said things like that to her, and with that same look in his eye, as if he was telling her the gospel truth and he thought she was too stupid to know it.

'Where's Jack now?' she demanded after a moment.

'Out with that young Dennis doing a test run. They drove off about ten minutes ago. Shouldn't be long.'

She looked at him, then nodded, turned and went outside. It

had been worrying her for a few weeks now, why Jack should all of a sudden give up bothering her for sex. It must've been — a month or more! she suddenly realised, since he'd last tried it on. She paused before going through the rear door of the garage and looked back thoughtfully at the butcher's shop. Old Sam, in his time, had been a one for a nice little bit of extra skirt. Her mother used to say it wasn't safe to be left alone in the same room with him; that he couldn't keep his horrible, smelly hands to himself. Thought he was Rudolf Valentino . . .

Jack had thought he was God's gift to women. Probably still did, for all she knew. She remembered how her girlfriends used to laugh at him behind his back. They'd thought she was mad for fancying him; that she must've been really hard up to want to go out with him and then spend the evening fighting him off. It was strange about that, how prim and proper he was during their courtship, she reflected. Despite what the other girls had warned her about him. Never so much as brushed his hand against her breast or put a hand on her leg, let alone tried to get her in the back seat of his car with her knickers off, the way they'd said he would, the first chance he got.

She paused just inside the garage door; thought about the times he was missing from the garage lately when she phoned down expecting that he would be there. There was last Saturday, Wednesday afternoon of last week — and now she came to think of it, the Wednesday afternoon of the week before that! Her wide brow wrinkled with the effort of thought. A month or more, that was how long it had been going on. Ever since he'd stopped bothering her!

He was getting it somewhere else! she realised with a shock.

Her mother had warned her that this was the sort of thing men did . . . if you wouldn't give them what they wanted.

But where? With whom? Who'd look twice at that bald head and revolting beer-gut?

Her eyes darkened with fury. He wouldn't dare. She'd kill him first!

She turned quickly; left the garage by the rear door. Her

husband's car was parked out the back and she went over to it. She didn't know what to expect, what she thought she was going to find; it was just that the things her girl-friends used to say to her about him — the things he got up to with girls in the back of his dad's butcher's van, and later on, when he was able to afford it, a car of his own — were suddenly foremost in her mind.

And here it was, the scene of the crime, waiting for her to go over it with a fine-tooth comb for the evidence of his guilt.

She looked through the car window at the back seat. If she had hoped to find a piece of women's intimate underclothing carelessly abandoned somewhere there, then she was to be disappointed. Everything looked exactly as it should. No unusual stains on the upholstery . . .

She studied the area concerned; wondered if it was roomy enough to do the sort of thing she had in mind; doubted it. Jack was a big man; clumsy; needed plenty of space to manoeuvre.

Her expression hardened. This, of course, explained why he had needed the rug. Like that dirty old devil back there in the shop had said . . . The grass *was* damp and cold!

She opened the door of the car and savagely snatched the keys from the ignition, where her husband always left them during the day, and then stormed round to the boot and opened it up. She knew the rug would be there; that when she found the rug, it would give her all the evidence she needed to prove that he had been using it while he was with another woman.

She was right.

The rug was there.

And more.

So was the other woman.

Alison Cockburn's head peeped out coquettishly from the folds of the rug. Her eyes stared boldly straight into Sylvia's. It registered on the periphery of Sylvia's mind that Alison was a funny colour, but this was all.

Momentarily incapable of thinking clearly, blind with rage, Sylvia snatched up a corner of the rug and wrenched it away from Alison with a choked roar.

Alison was completely naked except for the pair of nylon tights wrapped round her throat like a comforter.

It was almost as if Sylvia either didn't notice or found nothing at all odd about the part of her anatomy that Alison had chosen to wear her tights. Sylvia stood her ground defiantly, as if waiting for the girl to say something and make some attempt to cover up her shame.

Alison didn't move. Her eyes continued to stare at Sylvia until they became magnified, grew out of all proportion to the woman looking into them. Sylvia's blood turned suddenly to ice.

Sam Graves, in the butcher's shop, put down his mug of tea, looked thoughtfully round and wondered about his daughter-in-law, what the hell she thought she was going to find next door. He was surprised that she had condescended to go anywhere near the place. She wasn't interested in the garage; never had been; was forever on at Jack to sell it.

Sylvia continued to look woodenly down at Alison. She made not a sound and was still standing there looking at the girl when her husband and Dennis Pendlebury returned to the garage a full two minutes later.

Dennis gave Jack Graves, who was driving the car they had been checking out on the road, a startled look when he saw Sylvia. Dennis couldn't believe his eyes. He couldn't remember ever having seen Sylvia Graves anywhere near the garage. The other end of the telephone line was as near as she ever got to it, and he couldn't think what had brought her out the back.

Jack Graves had gone a terrible colour, a deathly white. He was staring at his wife, at the raised boot of the car on which one of her hands was still resting; knew what she had found in there.

He parked the car; hurried over to her.

She didn't see him for a moment; couldn't take her eyes from Alison's. Then, sensing her husband's presence at her side rather than actually seeing him, she turned her head slowly and looked at him; opened her mouth wide and screeched at him like a fishwife. A man and two elderly women, who were engaged in conversation outside the butcher's shop, paused and looked round quickly. A terrible silence hung on the air. The man in the street hesitated, frowned to himself as his mind replayed that ghastly, blood-curdling sound he had heard seconds earlier, then he went running round to the back of the garage to investigate.

Jack Graves looked into the boot, into the eyes of the naked girl who was staring accusingly at him. Then he turned and strode away, pushed past Dennis and the man from the street (who was standing uncertainly beside Dennis, a bemused expression on his face), burst through the back door of the butcher's shop, roughly brushed his father aside as the old man was about to step outdoors to see what was going on, rushed straight upstairs, got his shot-gun from the cupboard on the landing, loaded it quickly, put it to his mouth and pulled the trigger.

CHAPTER EIGHTEEN

Cyril Forbes was released from police custody early the following day, and as his sister had expected, was none the worse for his ordeal. In fact, twenty-four hours from now and she knew that the whole unfortunate matter would have been all but erased from his mind forever; recalled with only the greatest of difficulties. Cyril, Mrs Charles thought reflectively as she studied him later that same day, was one of those rare individuals who never wasted a moment's thought on what might have been. It was always the moment that counted with Cyril. And at that moment, he was sitting forward on her sofa, his kneecaps gripped tightly in his hands, the expression on his face that of a child anxious to be told he was excused and could go out and play.

'I never saw him, Graves,' said Cyril. 'I only saw Miss Sayer and that woman who looked over Roper's wall. Do the police know if Graves saw me?'

His sister shook her head. 'That's something nobody will ever know now,' she said. 'If Jack Graves did see you, then he apparently made no mention of it to Beryl Fisher. He couldn't, of course; not without running the risk of giving himself away about his having been on or near your property earlier than arranged with her, which was close to the time that Judith Caldicott was murdered, anyway.'

'So he was the one who rang you up pretending to be Judith's father, knowing that when she got here to your home to see you that afternoon and found you out, she'd come to me and ask where you were. Only when she got to my place, she found Graves waiting for her there instead of me.'

Mrs Charles nodded. 'The police have pieced together his movements that afternoon as best they can in the circumstances, and from what Dennis Pendlebury was able to tell them, they know that Graves left the garage on Wednesday afternoon soon after lunch — somewhere around two p.m. He didn't say where he was going: however, Beryl Fisher has told the police that her usual arrangement with Graves was that they'd meet at Whitethatch Cottage somewhere around three o'clock — an hour or thereabouts after Dennis said Graves left the garage that afternoon. Beryl is unsure of the exact time that either one of them arrived at the cottage last Wednesday afternoon, but she's told the police she's certain that it wasn't before three o'clock, and says it could've been nearer to three-thirty. Which gave Graves ample time, after leaving the garage at around two o'clock, to drive the long way into Gidding, and then back along the motorway so as to arrive at your house in time to open the front door to Judith when she drove on from here at three o'clock. He was using the two properties in the village where he thought there was absolutely no risk of his being disturbed by anyone. Whitethatch Cottage for his clandestine meetings with Beryl Fisher, knowing that the cottage has been empty for years; and your house for Judith Caldicott, which he knew would be deserted because, as everyone in the village knows, you always spend Wednesday shut up in the oast-house.'

'Do you think he planned to kill her?'

Mrs Charles shook her head. 'I shouldn't have thought so. From the stories that are circulating round the village at the moment about Jack Graves, and taking into consideration the number of affairs he's had with young local girls over the years that are suddenly coming to light and that apparently ran their course and then fizzled out, I'd say he merely wanted an opportunity to get Judith, the voluptuous sex goddess he'd watched on television — whom he may have seen as the ultimate catch — alone somewhere with him, and then try and work his magic charm on her. The only trouble was that in the event, it would seem that she was far from charmed — in her frame of mind, was probably very angry, if not a little hysterical. She may have even made some threat to him over the deceptive trick he'd played on her, and me, and said she was going to inform the police. Or worse, his wife! And from there things got tragically out of hand.'

'Never figured him for the cruel and violent sort. Or a womaniser. Always had his head buried in the engine of a car whenever I saw him; never seemed to have time for anything else.'

Mrs Charles shrugged. 'He was a butcher, like his father; and they themselves kill most of the meat they sell in their shop — which is obviously where he acquired his anatomical skills — so there would have to be a reasonably hard and unemotional streak in him.'

'Yes, but cutting the girl's vocal chords was carrying things a bit far, wasn't it?'

'Not if she mocked him in some way over his manhood. Judith had come up in a tough school. She was accustomed to giving as good as she got, and wouldn't hesitate to attack verbally, and in no uncertain terms, anyone who'd angered her in some way.'

Cyril eyed her speculatively. 'Graves was the peeping Tom somebody spotted skulking about one night at the back of her parents' home, and the bloke who stole her brassiere from off her mother's washing-line?'

'It would seem so,' she replied. 'He must've been fantasising about her ever since he first noticed her driving through the village in that expensive little car of hers.'

'Pity she didn't come the other way round, along the motorway, and then he might never have known anything about her visits to you.'

Mrs Charles looked thoughtful. 'That's hard to say. Village gossip being what it is, it would've been only a matter of time before somebody saw her calling on me and spread the word around. She came the long way through the village because she'd only recently passed her driving test and been given a driver's licence, and she didn't feel terribly confident as yet about driving on the motorway and tried to avoid it wherever she could.'

'Well, what about Alison Cockburn and him? How long had that been going on?'

'For some time, apparently. On his part, anyway; which makes her murder an even bigger tragedy. There was some forewarning of what was to come there; but unfortunately, Richard — one of Alison's brothers (the one with the bright pink cheeks and very fair hair) — who knew that Jack Graves was forcing his attentions on her, never thought to say anything to anybody about it until it was too late. Being very young (he's only eleven), Richard got things rather muddled and thought his sister was upset because she was hopelessly in love with Graves, whereas in actual fact, it was because he kept making unwelcome sexual advances to her. Her fiancé, Dennis Pendlebury, knew that Graves had been pestering Alison, but for fear of risking his job, and particularly now that he and Alison were getting married, he couldn't do anything about it other than to tell Alison to keep well away from the garage and to try and avoid being alone with the man as much as she could.'

Cyril was quiet for a moment. Then, with one of his brooding looks, he said, 'How do you account for her murder? I can accept that he got a bit carried away with Judith and killed her without necessarily meaning to, but to kill *twice* — and within a matter of days?'

'Well, as David Sayer remarked to me, the Jack the Rippers of this world who go round killing young women have to start somewhere, and if an opportunity presents itself, are hardly likely to hesitate about taking it, especially if they think they've got away with murder once. They become very confident — over-confident to the point of taking enormous risks, which Graves did when he used the same ploy and cancelled Alison's appointment with Mrs Blackmore, in this instance to give him time to set up his alibi and distance himself from the spot where Alison was last seen alive.'

Cyril looked doubtful. 'So he drives past Miss Sayer's cottage —'

Mrs Charles nodded; took up the narrative: '— With something rigged up in the front passenger-seat to block off an uninterrupted side view of the person sitting at the wheel, the police now think. The Jacksons' car was bought on the

Continent and is a left-hand drive, and although the risk at the time was slight because it was overcast and raining heavily, there was a possibility that Miss Sayer, if she was using her binoculars, would spot that it was Graves who was driving the car and not Mr Jackson. Graves was not to know, of course, that Miss Sayer was friendly with the Jacksons and knew that their car was in his garage being repaired, and that he'd arranged with Mr Jackson that he'd return it to him in Gidding on Saturday.'

Cyril fixed his dark eyes on his sister challengingly. 'You're saying he'd planned that far ahead what he was going to do with Alison Cockburn?'

Mrs Charles sighed. 'That's something else we'll never know for sure. David said there are a number of grey areas that the police aren't as happy with as they'd like to be, but with Graves dead, there's not going to be a lot that they can do about getting a clearer picture of what exactly went on, both in Graves's mind, and on Saturday afternoon. Beryl Fisher apparently contacted Graves at the garage first thing on Thursday morning in a state of panic about their having been together at Whitethatch Cottage the previous afternoon when Judith Caldicott was murdered, and he told her that he couldn't talk on the phone, it was too risky, and agreed with her that he'd meet her again at the cottage on Saturday. (He knew that the Jacksons were bringing their car in later that day, on the Thursday, and he said he'd be able to use the Jacksons as an excuse to get away for a time on Saturday.) He promised Beryl that they'd decide between them then what they were going to do should you suddenly remember having seen them on the previous Wednesday afternoon at the cottage and put either one of their names forward as witnesses to your whereabouts that afternoon.'

Cyril nodded, and after a slight pause, Mrs Charles continued:

'However, before setting out for Gidding and his meeting with Beryl on Saturday, Graves had to give the Jacksons' car a final road test to make sure that everything was all right with it. He knew that Alison had an appointment in the afternoon at the vicarage to discuss the floral arrangements for her wedding — I think just about everybody in the village knew about it — and it would seem that he simply couldn't resist making the most of the opportunity, particularly since he'd be out test driving one of his customer's cars at the time. He took a terrible risk, but men like him do take risks, more and more of them until finally, one day, they do it once too often and they're caught.'

She hesitated; looked pensive. 'The police think he must've caught up with Alison somewhere along the lane leading to the vicarage — an umbrella which Mr Mortimer had loaned her because it looked like rain, was found in a ditch at the side of the lane not far from the vicarage. Then somehow Graves enticed her into the car with him. It was raining heavily around that time and perhaps this was why she got into the Jacksons' car with him. They drove somewhere together — perhaps to Whitethatch Cottage (it was still too early for him to meet Beryl), or maybe he simply turned off the lane and pulled up somewhere and that was where he tried to force himself on her. Alison resisted, quite forcibly, and died — not of strangulation, but of heart failure. She was so terrified of him that she literally died of fright. The tights that were found round her throat were wrapped there by him later, after she was dead. Then he bundled her into the boot of the car (the police have found several strands of her hair in it), and drove back to the garage, reported to Dennis that the car was fine; and then a short while later, he set off for Gidding, again in the Jacksons' car, and had his meeting with Beryl at Whitethatch Cottage. In the meanwhile, however, he'd transferred Alison's body into the boot of his own car, wrapping it in a travelling-rug which Beryl has identified as being the one that was used while he was out and about on his amorous adventures with her.'

'How come young Pendlebury saw nothing of this?' asked Cyril.

'He was working under a car all afternoon trying to get it finished before knocking off time that evening. Graves simply came and stood beside the car Dennis was working on (Dennis only saw Graves's feet and legs: he was busy and didn't bother to come out from under the car). Graves reported that the Jacksons' car seemed all right to him, and then he disappeared for a time — obviously to shift Alison's body before taking the Jacksons' car back to them and meeting Beryl. Dennis gave him no more thought until Mrs Graves started pestering him about her husband's whereabouts, and then Dennis began to get suspicious and guessed that the reason Graves was so late in getting back was because he was meeting one of his girl-friends again. Which is exactly what he was doing. He met Beryl as agreed between them, they talked things over; decided not to do anything precipitous, that they should wait and see what happened. Then they both drove separately into Gidding. Graves dropped the Jacksons' car off (popping the keys of the car through the letter-box as arranged with them) while Beryl waited for him out of sight, then she drove him back to the outskirts of the village where he picked up a bus and continued the journey home.'

'He took a chance leaving the girl's body in the boot of his car, didn't he?'

'He obviously thought not. I've only ever seen him in his car: I don't think Mrs Graves ever went out anywhere in it with him. It was one of those million to one chances, like your coming out of the oast-house on Wednesday. Mrs Graves decided to launder some blankets before winter sets in, and she needed the travelling-rug to replace one of them temporarily. She couldn't find it anywhere in the house, so she asked her father-in-law if he knew where it was, and he told her that he'd seen his son go through to the garage carrying a travelling-rug some weeks ago. She then went outside and looked in the car and discovered Alison's body wrapped up in the rug in the boot. Mrs Graves has told the police that if her husband hadn't shot himself, she would've. Actually seemed a little disappointed, David said, that her husband had cheated her of the pleasure!'

'I've always thought she was a bit unhinged,' remarked Cyril.

'Yes, she's a strange woman. But then again, there can be

little doubt that her husband was a sexual deviant and impotent — neither girl was sexually molested — and wives and mothers are not usually the last to know of these things. This may explain her attitude towards him.'

'Do you think she's had her suspicions and been covering up for him?'

'Perhaps not knowingly: but I can't believe she didn't know that he was impotent and sexually deviant.'

Cyril's dark eyes regarded her interrogatively. 'But not with Beryl Fisher? They had normal sexual relations with one another?'

Mrs Charles looked at her brother for a moment. Then nodded and said, 'Apparently. Though David said that from her account of the relationship, it would seem that they were both somewhat naive sexually. If she's telling the truth, of course. With no one to contradict her, who's to say what really went on out there in the cottage between them?'

They sat for a moment in silence, then Cyril nodded his head and said, 'The bolts on the front forks weren't properly tightened, that's why she was so upset.' Then, rising to his feet, he crossed to the door.

His sister called him back. 'What on earth are you talking about, Cyril?'

He looked round at her over his shoulder. 'You wanted to know, didn't you?'

She looked at him blankly. Then her expression suddenly cleared and she nodded her head quickly and said, 'Oh, that . . . The motor bike Barry Edmonds was riding when he was killed. I'd forgotten all about it. Mr Merton gave you my message, then?'

Cyril said, 'Judith was upset and crying at choir practice one night. Everybody — all the girls were crying. Nearly drove me mad! She said the garage who'd fixed the boy's bike after it had broken down, hadn't done the job properly.'

'Was there any truth in this, do you think?'

'I don't know. She never talked to me about it. It was one of the other girls who told me what was the matter with everybody, why all the girls were upset.'

She eyed him thoughtfully. 'So you did know Barry Edmonds after all?'

He considered the question; shrugged. 'I think he left the choir the year I took over from Wilkins as choirmaster. Edmonds jacked it in when his voice broke.'

'Ah, so he was the boy with the voice of a bullfrog you wished would go and sit in some other pond and do his croaking?'

'Who was that?' asked Cyril.

'You told me about him yesterday,' she reminded him.

'Did I?'

'Yes, Cyril.'

'Couldn't have been Edmonds.'

'Why not?'

'He would've been a lot older than Judith. had to be if he was old enough to be riding a motor bike when he was killed. I'm not sure exactly how old she was at the time, but it couldn't have been much more than thirteen or fourteen. All the youngsters in the choir were around that age, or within a couple of years either side of it. Edmonds must've been at least eighteen when he died.'

'Yes, of course,' she said in a thoughtful voice. 'Somehow I've always imagined him as having been a much younger person . . . nearer to Judith's age, whereas he was obviously a good few years older than she was. Perhaps as much as five years older.' She sighed. 'Well, anyway, that's that mystery cleared up.'

'What's that?'

'Alison's reference to the motor bike in her note to me. She knew that Judith believed the accident was caused through negligence on the part of the garage where Barry Edmonds's bike was fixed, and she expected that Judith's uncle — being a policeman — would know about it and that he'd be able to give me all the details if I asked him for them.'

'I don't follow you.'

'The garage concerned, Cyril. It must've been Graves's Garage; and if my memory serves me correctly, at the time of the accident, Jack Graves would've been working entirely on his own in the garage, part-time and in between helping his father out in the butcher's shop. It's only been in these past few years that business has picked up and he's needed help.'

'You mean Graves deliberately didn't do a proper job on the boy's bike so that the boy would have a serious accident on it?'

'I think Alison — and Judith — might've thought so.'

'Why would Graves do a thing like that?'

'I think the answer to that is obvious, don't you? Correct me if I'm wrong, but Judith was always a precocious girl, sexually mature beyond her years. She probably came over here to the garage on the back of her boy-friend's bike at one time or another, and as far back as then, Jack Graves set his sights on her; and resenting the youthful opposition, Barry Edmonds, took what steps he could to eliminate him when a suitable opportunity presented itself.'

'The man must've been mad!' he muttered.

Yes, thought Mrs Charles with a slight shiver. *A highly dangerous psychopath, to say the very least!*

She sighed and her brother, who was standing in the doorway watching her, asked, 'What's wrong?'

'Nothing, really.' She smiled at him. 'But you know what I'm like about loose ends.'

'What loose ends? I can't see any.'

'You, Cyril: you're the one loose end that still bothers me.'

He looked alarmed. 'You're not going to tell me that you've got another one of your funny feelings, are you?'

She thought for a moment. 'I'm not sure . . . I can't help feeling that something's very wrong; that I'm missing something.' She looked at her brother then shook her head regretfully. 'I'm sorry, Cyril, but I have to say it. It's you. Your story — your alibi, if you like — simply doesn't fit, and I'll be frank with you, I'm not satisfied; I think you've still got a lot of explaining to do. You're going to have to go right back to the beginning and start all over again!'

CHAPTER NINETEEN

Thin sunlight slanted through the stained-glass windows of the hushed church and lay across the coffin resting on its bier before the steps leading up to the chancel. By request, there were no floral tributes other than for what should have been Alison Cockburn's bridal bouquet of small, creamy-white roses which lay on the lid of her coffin. Tilly Cockburn was leaning heavily against her husband and weeping softly onto his shoulder. On her other side, Dennis Pendlebury, ashen-faced, his head bowed, supported her with his arm. Alison's younger sister, Kathleen, and her brothers, Harry and Melville, stood in a huddled, miserable line at their father's side. Richard Cockburn, white-faced and stiff-shouldered, stood apart from the rest of his family as though cast out by them. Mrs Charles's gaze lingered on him for a moment. His isolation from the other members of the Cockburn family heightened his grief and the guilt he felt (or was perhaps being made to feel by his family over the part he had played in his sister's death), which was etched sharply into every contour of his small, tense frame. He, more than any other member of his family, or Dennis Pendlebury, made a truly pitiful sight, which Mrs Charles found profoundly disturbing. She sincerely hoped that if the child were being shunned deliberately by his family, they would soon find it in their hearts to forgive and forget before, overwhelmed by guilt and grief, he was driven to punish himself in some way; quite possibly, with tragic consequences.

The Reverend Frank Blackmore was thanking God for the privilege He had given the Cockburn family, Alison's fiancé, Dennis, and the people of Little Gidding in allowing them to have known and loved the deceased young woman for the all too brief time she had lived and worked among them.

At these words, the young girl sharing the same pew as Mrs Charles and David Sayer, broke into loud, hacking sobs that filled the large old Norman church and completely drowned out the Reverend Blackmore's quiet, solemn voice.

Mrs Charles looked at the girl thoughtfully. She was to have been one of Alison's bridesmaids, and of everybody in the packed church, many of whom were now visibly in tears, she was the most audibly distressed.

David followed Mrs Charles's gaze, then gave her a bemused look and mouthed, '*Who's that?*'

Mrs Charles turned her head from the girl. 'Carol Roper,' she replied in a soft undertone.

The funeral service came to a close and the mourners filed silently out into St Stephen's tiny churchyard for the final burial rites at the graveside.

Half an hour later, Mrs Charles and David walked slowly away from the church towards his aunt's cottage.

Ahead of them was Richard Cockburn. The rest of his family, together with Dennis Pendlebury and his mother, had returned to the Cockburns' home on the other side of the village, in the long black limousines provided by the funeral directors.

'I promised my aunt I'd sit with her until Mrs Pendlebury gets back,' said David. 'The old girl'll be gasping for her cup of tea. You'll come in and join us, won't you?'

'No, thank you all the same,' she replied, an anxious eye on the back of the boy walking ahead of them. 'I'd like to have a talk with Richard.'

David looked at the boy. 'Poor kid. He's taking it hard.'

'Too hard,' said Mrs Charles with a worried shake of her head.

Richard paused and turned when Mrs Charles called his name.

'Hello, Richard,' she said, walking up to him. 'Getting a breath of fresh air?'

He nodded and they fell into step alongside one another.

'Are you going somewhere special?' she asked him after a moment.

He shook his head. They had reached her front gate and they paused. 'Would you like to come inside for a glass of milk and some chocolate cake?' she asked him.

He shook his head again. If anything, his face had grown even whiter, his lips thinner.

'Well, then,' she said with a gentle smile, 'would you like to come in and just sit quietly for a little while?'

He nodded; followed her up the path and indoors; sat, without speaking, on the sofa in her sitting-room with his kneecaps clasped tightly in his hands the way her brother would sit when he had something weighing heavily on his mind, and stared straight ahead of him. Mrs Charles ignored him; took off her gloves and coat and then sat down opposite him.

They continued to sit quietly together in the lengthening shadows of the afternoon. Then, rising finally to switch on a table-lamp, Mrs Charles said, 'Richard, do you think it would be a good idea if I telephoned your mother to let her know where you are?'

'She won't care,' he muttered. 'They don't care if I live or die. They all hate me. It's my fault Alison's dead. I killed her. That's what they all think.'

She didn't argue with him; nodded her head sympathetically.

He went on, 'They wouldn't have believed me if I'd told.' His small jaw set grimly. 'They never believe anything I say. They're always telling me to shut up and to stop making things up, and to go upstairs to my room.'

He stood up abruptly. He was close to tears; struggling to control himself. 'I think I'd like to go now.'

Mrs Charles said, 'No, please don't go just yet, Richard. Sit down for a minute — You've got a minute you can spare me, haven't you? There's something very important I want to discuss with you. I need your help very badly.'

He looked at her, hesitated, then sat down again.

'But first,' she went on with another gentle smile, 'I really think we should let your mother know where you are, don't you? Then we'll go out to the kitchen and get something to eat and we'll have our little talk.'

He looked at her hesitantly, then nodded his consent to these arrangements.

He declined to eat or drink anything when they went through to the kitchen a few minutes later; sat down stiffly on the chair Mrs Charles offered him, then gazed past her out of the window at nothing.

'Richard,' she said after a moment. 'Do you know who I am, how I earn my living?'

He flicked his eyes at her, then returned his gaze to the window. 'You tell fortunes,' he said.

'That's right. What else?'

His eyes flicked at her again. 'Mum said you sometimes help the police with their murder cases.'

She nodded. 'Yes — sometimes on my own, but usually with Mr Sayer's help. You know who Mr Sayer is, of course.'

He nodded. 'He used to be a policeman.'

She said, 'Well, this time, Richard, Mr Sayer can't help me with the case I'm working on. And I can't solve it on my own. I need someone to help me. This case is far too big for me to handle all alone — the biggest I've ever tackled. I might not even be able to solve it; that's if I can't find someone who's willing to help me work on it.'

The boy looked at her; made no comment.

She looked at him gravely. 'Can you keep a secret, Richard?' she asked. 'A very big secret — one you must promise me will be *our* secret, just between the two of us? You understand that if you agree to work with me on this case, it must be in strictest confidence?'

He thought about it; nodded.

'Very well, then: what I specially want to talk to you about is the letter you mentioned the other day while I was visiting your mother. The one you told me you saw Alison writing to Mr Graves.'

The boy's mouth set stubbornly. 'She did write a letter; I saw her! She hid it. I saw her hide it. She told me a fib: she said she was making a list of the people she was going to invite to her wedding. But that isn't true; she did that ages ago. She *was* writing a letter. I didn't make it up. I was telling the truth.'

'Yes, I know you were, Richard.'

He looked at her, bemused.

Mrs Charles reached up to a shelf on her dresser and took down Alison's note to her; handed it to him.

'Does this look like the letter you saw Alison writing in her room?'

He read it; looked up from it into Mrs Charles's face. 'That's not to Mr Graves: that's not to anybody.'

'It is the letter, though? The one you saw her writing?'

He nodded.

'Well, Richard; the truth is, Alison was writing to me.'

His very clear blue eyes clouded with puzzlement.

Mrs Charles continued, 'That was why she was coming to see me as soon as she'd finished talking to Mrs Blackmore at the vicarage about the flowers for the church. Alison was going to tell me what this letter is all about.'

The boy looked at her; his expression was solemn. 'You mean she had some information to assist you in your inquiries,' he said after a moment.

Mrs Charles nodded her head.

'Alison was working undercover with you — like Mr Sayer does?'

'In a way, yes . . . I suppose she was. That's why it's so very important that you keep our secret about our little talk this afternoon. It could be very dangerous for us if the wrong person finds out that we're working together.'

The expression in his eyes sharpened measurably. 'Is this why Alison was killed? It didn't have anything to do with Mr Graves after all?'

'This is what I want to try and find out, Richard. With your help, of course.' She paused; frowned a little. 'You can understand how very upset I'm feeling about this. I feel it's my fault that Alison was killed . . . because I knew about the letter and that you were telling the truth, and because I didn't back you up and tell somebody about it.'

The boy looked concerned. 'It wasn't your fault: you didn't know, did you? You can't be blamed. It was just bad luck,' he said, his tone very serious. 'Alison knew too much. She had to be shut up.'

'Will you help me to find out for sure what really happened to her, Richard? If it was my fault that she was killed?'

He nodded.

'Good,' she said. She smiled at him. 'I feel much better already. Now, let's get back to this letter . . .' She took it from the boy; pored over it for a moment. 'It's the only real clue we've got to work on, Richard. Let's make a list, shall we?'

She got a notepad and pencil, then held the pencil ready, as if poised to take dictation from him.

'We'll start with you,' she said. 'You knew about the letter — that your sister had written to somebody — though you, of course, mistakenly thought that person was Mr Graves when she was really writing to me —' (she waited for his response and after pondering for a moment, the boy nodded) — 'I know this,' she went on as she wrote down his name, 'because you told me about it, and your mother, the day I called to see her and you were at home with a sore throat.'

Carefully, he turned all of this over in his mind, then nodded. 'Yes, but none of us killed Alison, did we? We are in the clear.'

'Yes,' agreed Mrs Charles. 'So that means it had to be somebody else — some other person who knew about the letter.' She paused. 'Who else besides you and I and your mother (and Alison, of course) knew about the letter, Richard?'

He shook his head. 'Nobody else.'

'Think very hard, Richard. It's very important that you should be absolutely certain of this. It's the only way we are going to get to the bottom of this mystery.'

He looked at her hesitantly. 'Well . . . Carol Roper — Sort of. We were teasing her.'

'Who is *we*, Richard?'

'Me and her brothers and sisters and some of the other kids.' Richard looked at her earnestly. 'Carol's madly in love with

Mr Graves, too. That's why she was so upset in church; because he's dead. She's going to have a baby; that's why Alison went mad at her for getting too big round the tummy to fit into her bridesmaid's dress. I heard Alison telling her off. They were up in Alison's bedroom trying on their dresses. Alison said Carol would have to go on a crash diet because it was too late to get the dress made any bigger. But that wouldn't do any good, would it? Carol's pregnant,' he added, with careful emphasis on the word *pregnant*, as if using it for the first time.

Mrs Charles was cutting him a slice of chocolate cake. She inched it towards him, then poured him a glass of milk.

'Go on, Richard; I'm listening. Who else did you tell besides Carol Roper?'

CHAPTER TWENTY

Mrs Charles was waiting for Carol at the bus-stop at the top of the road when Carol returned home from her office job in Gidding the following evening.

The girl looked pale and drawn and was so preoccupied with her thoughts as she stepped down from the bus, that she neither noticed Mrs Charles nor heard her speak.

She looked up with a start when she suddenly became aware of the older woman and realised that she was speaking to her.

'Oh,' she said quickly. Then, a second time: 'Oh . . . Mrs Charles. I didn't see you. You startled me. I'm sorry, I didn't catch what you said.'

Mrs Charles gave her a friendly smile. 'I'm sorry to trouble you, Carol,' she said. 'But do you think you could spare me a few minutes? I've something very important I'd like to discuss with you.'

The girl looked puzzled. In common with the other young woman who had apparently been smitten with Jack Graves (assuming, of course, that the information Richard Cockburn had given Mrs Charles about Carol Roper and the village garage proprietor had at least a grain of truth in it), she was not an attractive-looking girl; completely lacking in colour and personality — even more so, thought Mrs Charles, than Beryl Fisher — which made her sonorous display of grief at her friend's funeral service all the more remarkable, and suggestive, Mrs Charles felt, of something far more intimately personal, something which grieved and distressed Carol and which concerned Carol and Carol alone. It was not that Mrs Charles doubted the girl's sorrow at her friend's death; she simply knew instinctively from her long professional experience with severely emotionally distressed and troubled people, that for some reason, Alison's death had magnified and intensified some deeply personal problem of her own, and that the girl was also weeping for herself. The claim Richard had made about her, if it were true, would be one reason for her to feel desperately sorry for herself, but there was every possibility that Richard had once again got all his facts muddled and that there was something else troubling her, something completely removed from the tragedy which had befallen her friend and the subsequent suicide of Jack Graves; and one way or another Mrs Charles was determined to find out what it was. She had to find out, had to be sure that these nagging doubts of hers over that one curious anomaly in her brother's statement to the police, had no substance to them.

'Is there somewhere we could talk?' asked Mrs Charles. 'Privately, that is.'

The girl stared at her.

Mrs Charles looked at her gravely. 'It's about your friendship with Mr Graves, Carol.'

The girl's face whitened; her eyes widened in alarm. 'I — I don't know what you're talking about,' she stammered.

'I think you do, Carol.' Mrs Charles spoke quietly. 'Beryl Fisher wasn't the only young girl from the village who was meeting Mr Graves secretly out at Whitethatch Cottage, was she?'

'We never went —' The girl broke off; looked slightly sick. 'I've got nothing to say. I don't know anything about Mr Graves. I've got to go; I'll be late for my tea.'

'Very well, Carol: I'll say no more about the matter for now. You know where to find me, that's if you ever feel you'd like someone to talk to about your troubles.'

'What troubles?' asked the girl. She looked at Mrs Charles defiantly. 'I haven't got any troubles. You're nothing but a horrible old busybody. I'm going to —'

'Yes, Carol?' Mrs Charles looked at her steadily; spoke firmly. 'What are you going to do? Tell your parents? The police, perhaps?' The clairvoyant paused. Then, in a softer voice, she said, 'I don't really think that will be necessary, you know; not if you're sensible about this and you tell me all that you know about Mr Graves and Alison Cockburn. There may still be some way we can keep your name out of this. And your relationship with Mr Graves.'

The girl blenched; turned quickly and hurried away in the direction of her father's dairy.

Mrs Charles went home and waited. It was getting on for eleven o'clock when Carol's knock finally came at her door and for a moment, Mrs Charles thought she might be mistaken, that the girl wasn't coming to see her after all, it was Cyril making a late night call on her.

Carol said at first that she wouldn't come inside; then, as if suddenly remembering Miss Sayer's cottage, that the old lady might be able to see her standing in Mrs Charles's porch-light and wonder what was going on, she glanced back along the road and quickly changed her mind.

'I only wanted to tell you that there must be some mistake,' said the girl. 'I couldn't come before, I had to wait until Mum and Dad went to bed.' She spoke sullenly; looked disgruntled. 'I don't know anything about Alison and Mr Graves. I don't know why you should think I'd know anything about them. I don't know who's been telling you these things about me and Alison, but they're not true. Alison didn't like him. She was always telling me —'

'— That you were a very foolish girl for getting involved with him, a married man?' suggested Mrs Charles. Then, in response to the angry look the girl gave her: 'I'm not going to preach at you, Carol. All I want is the truth.'

'Why should I talk to you?' The girl's face reddened with anger; her eyes were wide and staring. 'It's none of your business!'

'I'm afraid that's exactly what it is, Carol. My brother's good name in this village is my business.'

'What's he got to do with this?' the girl muttered, glowering sullenly at Mrs Charles.

'A certain statement that my brother made to the police concerning Judith Caldicott's death makes him out to be a liar, despite the fact that he was innocent of her murder. I intend to clear his name completely by proving that at no time was he untruthful in any of the statements that he made to the police about Judith Caldicott's murder. However, in order to do this, you must first tell me the truth, all that you know about Alison and Mr Graves.'

'I don't know about any statement Mr Forbes made to the police. What's this got to do with me? And why do you keep saying that about Alison and Mr Graves?' Carol scowled irritably. 'I told you, she didn't like him. She — she used to go out of her way to avoid him.'

'Yes, exactly. So why then did she get into a car with him on Saturday afternoon?'

'She —' Carol broke off.

The expression in Mrs Charles's eyes hardened. 'Go on, Carol. You were saying?'

The girl shook her head; her face set determinedly. 'I'm not saying any more.'

'I warn you, Carol,' said Mrs Charles in a calm, firm voice. 'I'm going to get to the bottom of this, even if it means going to the police and telling them what I know, and then letting them ask you the questions which you seem so reluctant to answer for me. Do you really want Jack Graves, an innocent man perhaps, like my brother, to be damned for all eternity for something he might not have done?'

The girl was close to tears. 'I can't tell you,' she whimpered. 'Don't you understand? If I tell you it'll all have to come out; about me and him, and —'

'The baby you're expecting?'

The girl turned her head away, screwed up her eyes and started to cry. 'What am I going to do?' she wailed. 'If they find out — Mum and Dad — they'll throw me out, I know they will.'

'It isn't a problem that's just arisen, Carol. You've known for quite a while that you're pregnant, haven't you? What did you and Mr Graves propose to do about the situation? Did he promise to marry you?'

The girl looked back at her miserably; rubbed the tears from her eyes with the back of her hand. 'He — he wouldn't help me,' she said in a dull voice. 'He said he couldn't marry me, his wife wouldn't give him a divorce.'

'Had he asked her for one?'

The girl shook her head. 'We only talked about it on —' She gulped; dragged out her handkerchief and wiped her nose. She sniffed loudly. 'He said he'd give me some money to say the baby was someone else's. He said he had no guarantee the baby was his, anyway. But that isn't true.' She shook her head vigorously. 'It is his! I've never done it with anyone else, I swear it! I loved him, nobody else,' she wept bitterly. 'How could I have done that with somebody else when he was the one I loved?'

Mrs Charles sighed a little; rose from her chair.

The girl looked at her quickly. 'What — what are you going to do?' she stammered fearfully.

'I'm going to make you a cup of tea. You can come out to the kitchen with me if you like.'

Carol nodded; got swiftly to her feet and followed her out of the room.

'I can't stop worrying about it. What am I going to tell my Mum and Dad?' wailed the girl, slumping onto a chair in a fresh flood of tears.

'The truth, Carol. I think you already know that.'

'They'll throw me out, and then what'll I do? I've got no money; nowhere to go.'

'I know your parents; they'll be shocked, naturally, but once they've been given a little time to adjust to the situation, I'm sure they'll stand by you and give you the help and support you're going to need over the next few months. But if I'm wrong, then I promise that I'll help you and see to it that you're properly taken care of until your baby is born and you decide what you want for the future.'

The girl sniffed; watched Mrs Charles, who went on making the tea as if she were not there. After a moment or two, Carol sniffed again, then asked, 'What do you want to know?'

'I've told you, Carol. The truth about Alison and Mr Graves.'

'There's nothing more to tell.' The girl spoke wearily, as if all the fight had been drained out of her. 'I've told you everything I know. Honestly. Alison hated him.'

'Then why did she get into the Jacksons' car with him?'

'She — she didn't.'

Mrs Charles looked at Carol. 'What do you mean?'

Carol started to cry again. 'I don't know what I mean. I don't understand it. I've thought and thought about it, and I just don't understand it. I've wanted to talk to somebody about it, honestly I have; but I couldn't. You understand that, don't you? I couldn't tell anybody without — without them finding out about me — and him, Mr Graves. One minute I thought it was him, and the next I thought no, it couldn't be him. I was so confused. And frightened. Everybody seemed so sure he'd killed Alison. He killed himself, didn't he — because of the terrible thing he'd done? What if nobody believed me and — and . . . well, the moment I talked, he'd know, wouldn't he? The real killer. I mean, if there is one, somebody else, and it wasn't Mr Graves after all who killed Alison. He'd know I knew the truth. Then I'd be next, wouldn't I?' she sobbed. 'He'd have to kill me too, like all the others.'

Relieved at last to be sharing her doubts and fears with some other person, Carol went on speaking for quite some time, for the most part in an incoherent gabble.

Mrs Charles continued to listen to her without interrupting until the girl finally came to a choking halt, and then she said, 'Now, let me get this absolutely straight, Carol. You say you phoned Mr Graves at the garage on Saturday afternoon — somewhere around three o'clock, you think — and told him that if he didn't meet you straight away to get things sorted out between you concerning the child you're expecting, you were going to his wife and you'd tell her about your affair. You argued for a time, he tried to persuade you to wait a day or two because he was very busy that afternoon and couldn't afford

the time, but you remained adamant that you were going to
tell his wife about the two of you, and he finally agreed to meet
you. But not immediately. He said he'd have to wait until he
was sure that Alison was safely out of the way because he
didn't want her to see you together and perhaps mention it to
someone later on —'

Mrs Charles paused; looked puzzled. 'I'm sorry, Carol; all
of this seems perfectly simple and straightforward to me. What
is it exactly that you don't understand? Everything you've told
me ties in perfectly with the police reconstruction of the events
of that afternoon — with the exception of you, of course . . .
your involvement with Mr Graves. The police knew about
Beryl Fisher, but they didn't know there was a second girl he'd
also arranged to meet on Saturday afternoon. And from what
you've told me, I'd say you've merely strengthened Mr
Graves's motive for killing Alison. She was your best friend
and sooner or later — assuming she didn't already know about
the two of you and the baby that's on the way — she was
going to find out about everything and then there was every
chance that the story would be spread all round the village and
would eventually reach his wife's ears.'

Carol was shaking her head: she spoke impatiently. 'No . . .
Don't you see? It was the wrong car!'

Mrs Charles stared at her for a very long time without
saying anything, then gazed at the cup which a moment or two
earlier, Carol had covered quickly with her hand as Mrs
Charles had wordlessly offered to refill it from the teapot.

'You do see, don't you?' said the girl.

Mrs Charles nodded her head slowly. 'I'm not sure, but I
think I'm beginning to, Carol. And if I'm right in what I'm
thinking, then I'm very much afraid that your fears for your
safety are well founded. Particularly if Margaret Sayer's aware
that you've called to see me tonight.'

'Oh, her,' said the girl. She spoke disparagingly; her mouth
soured. 'That vicious old so-and-so never misses a trick!'

But that was just it, thought Mrs Charles, shocked. *Exactly
what the old lady had missed seeing. A very clever trick.*

Mrs Charles moved towards the door.

'Where are you going now?' demanded the girl, almost as if frightened to be left on her own.

'I have to speak to my brother,' said Mrs Charles.

'At this hour? What about?'

'A lie,' replied Mrs Charles in a thoughtful voice. 'And a very clever piece of sleight of hand . . . Something a magician does right under your nose without your knowing it.'

CHAPTER TWENTY-ONE

'This had better be good, Madame!' growled Merton. His light overcoat looked abnormally bulky and rumpled, as if he had carelessly pulled on all his clothes over his pyjamas because he did not propose to allow this interruption to his night's sleep to be of any great duration. 'You've disturbed the best night's rest I've had in weeks!'

'Not without due thought and consideration, I assure you, Mr Merton,' said Mrs Charles as he and David Sayer followed her into her sitting-room.

David glanced at her when he saw her brother waiting for them, but she ignored the question in his eyes.

Merton glowered at Cyril and curtly nodded his head. Cyril returned the greeting with one of his long, brooding looks. He was sitting well forward on the sofa with his kneecaps gripped tightly in his hands as usual, and again as if waiting to be told that he was excused and that he could go now.

'Now, what's this all about? And please be as brief as possible: I've got a heavy day ahead of me, and I would like to get a little more sleep before then, if you don't mind,' grumbled Merton.

He and David sat down in armchairs: Mrs Charles sat beside Cyril; as if, thought David, what she was about to tell them was going to be unpleasant for her brother, and she wished, by this one simple gesture, to convey to everyone in the room that she fully intended to stand by him and give him whatever moral support he needed.

'I am sure you recall the conversation that I had with my brother at his house the other morning,' she began.

Merton spoke dryly. 'As if I could forget it, Madame. Most informative.'

Mrs Charles smiled faintly at the sarcasm. 'Yes, quite: however, neither one of us — and I'm talking now about you and I — realised it at the time. As I left my brother's house that morning, you inquired whether he'd told me what I'd wanted to know; to which I replied, "Very probably." In actual fact, Mr Merton, although I didn't realise it myself at the time, Cyril had told me everything, the truth about who really killed Judith Caldicott. While I appreciate that it may not seem like it to you, Cyril doesn't deal in useless information. We may not understand the significance of the seemingly totally unconnected comments and remarks he makes (and I think he'll bear with me when I say that as often as not, neither does he!), but in the long run, they all prove to have a direct bearing on the subject that was actually under discussion when these obscure remarks of his were made.'

'Good,' said Merton, his tone drier than ever. 'I'm glad we've cleared up that little point.' He looked at her dourly. 'Surely all of this is academic now? We've got our man. Mr Forbes is completely in the clear so far as we're concerned.'

'But he's not, Mr Merton. That's just it. We still haven't cleared up the anomaly in his statement concerning his movements on Wednesday afternoon of last week.'

Merton stared at her; his face reddened. 'You've got me out of bed in the middle of the night to argue the toss with me about your brother's statement? Madame, I assure you — on behalf of myself, on behalf of the entire Gidding Constabulary (on behalf of the entire Nation, if you insist!), I could not care less where Mr Forbes was that Wednesday afternoon.'

'But I care, Mr Merton,' she said in a quiet, determined voice. 'And so should you. Because if we'd all looked at Cyril's statement about his movements that afternoon, if we'd looked for the lie then instead of later, Alison Cockburn would be alive today.'

Merton was about to make some sharp retort, but hesitated. He scowled at her. 'I've absolutely no idea what you're talking about, but I'll go along with you. So all right, your brother lied to everybody, and if we'd examined that lie we'd have arrived at the truth sooner and a girl's life would've been saved. But that wouldn't have altered the fact that Jack Graves was our man.'

'I didn't say my brother lied, Mr Merton,' said Mrs Charles. She looked at him gravely. 'I said we should've looked at his statement a little more closely. Cyril wasn't lying. He was telling the truth. Someone else was lying.'

David broke in with a frown. 'My aunt?' He looked startled.

'No,' she said. 'She was telling the truth, too. This was where we made our mistake: in not accepting from the beginning that both Miss Sayer and Cyril were telling the truth. Miss Sayer didn't see Cyril walk past her window that afternoon for the simple reason, I believe, that she dozed off and was asleep during those few vital minutes it took for him to walk along the road past her cottage and then disappear round the corner into Roper's road. This is, of course, a possibility we should've considered from the outset, bearing in mind Miss Sayer's advanced years; but we didn't, and the reason we didn't was because of her cup of afternoon tea . . . The cup of tea which Mrs Pendlebury brought in to Miss Sayer shortly after three o'clock. When Mrs Pendlebury returned later to collect Miss Sayer's cup, it was empty, and the natural conclusion Miss Sayer (and everyone else since) reached on seeing that empty cup was that she'd drunk the tea. But she hadn't.'

Mrs Charles turned to David. 'I'm sure you recall telling me that your wife, Jean, had made a comment to you that she'd noticed how rigid and fixed in her ways your aunt has become since Jean last visited her. You told me that one of the things that particularly irritates your aunt is to be offered more than one cup of tea; and yet, according to a conversation I've had with Mrs Pendlebury about Miss Sayer's statement concerning my brother that afternoon — the afternoon Cyril walked past Miss Sayer's window — Miss Sayer complained to Mrs Pendlebury of a thirst and requested a refill.'

Mrs Charles smiled faintly at the bemused expression on David's face. She went on, 'I think we should now seriously consider the possibility that the reason your aunt was so thirsty wasn't because it was an unusually warm day, but because she hadn't had anything at all to drink that afternoon. The very warm afternoon, and her prolonged inactivity, would also account for her feeling a little more drowsy than usual. Miss Sayer hadn't the faintest idea that she'd fallen asleep that afternoon — and I'd think for quite a good bit longer than for just a few minutes. She saw her empty cup and assumed she'd been sitting there quietly drinking her tea while watching the comings and goings of the people and cars moving along the road outside her cottage, as has been her custom these past few weeks while she's been waiting for her broken femur to mend.'

'All right, it's a possibility,' said Merton with an irritable scowl. 'So we've accounted for the discrepancy in Mr Forbes's statement. The old girl — er, Miss Sayer —' he put in, glancing apologetically at David '— dozed off for a time that afternoon. Is that it? I can go back home to bed now?'

Mrs Charles looked at him for a moment, then turned her head and gazed at her brother. She spoke musingly. 'Mrs Langston looked over Roper's wall and I'm convinced that she mistook Cyril for a cow. Cyril would be the last person she'd expect to see out and about on a Wednesday, so she simply didn't see him.' She looked back at Merton. 'And Mr North, our local weather-man, who I have no doubt did spend some time in Roper's field that day, was confused about his times, and was actually working in the wood at the bottom of my garden that afternoon and wouldn't have therefore seen Cyril.'

Merton looked at David, who shrugged his shoulders a little; looked equally bemused. Then Merton said, a shade sarcastically, 'If I apologise now, in person, to Mr Forbes for my having doubted his word, and then follow it up with a formal written apology, will that make amends? You're rather carrying things a bit far, aren't you, about this statement of Mr Forbes's?'

'I only wish I'd done it sooner,' said Mrs Charles. 'And it's not to Cyril that you — I — should apologise, Mr Merton. It's to Alison Cockburn's family. They are the ones who are paying the price for my mistake.'

'Your mistake, Madame?'

'Yes, this is my mistake, Mr Merton. You couldn't have been expected to know, as I should've known, that my brother was telling the absolute truth, and that because of this absolute truthfulness on his part, somewhere within the context of his statement to the police (as with the conversation he and I had at his house the other day), was the clue to the identity of the person who really killed Judith Caldicott, and who then killed Alison Cockburn, and who will now have to kill again, a third time. For want of a better description, Mr Merton, there's been only one sex crime, and that was the murder of Judith Caldicott. Alison's murder was a natural sequence of events. She knew something about Judith's past that could link Judith directly with her killer. The only trouble was, Alison didn't want to believe it — she desperately hoped she was wrong. Unfortunately, she herself proved that her worst fears were a reality when she too was murdered. And now another girl is likewise going to be murdered because of what she fears. This third girl knows nothing of Judith's murder, but she can help us to put the lie to who killed her best friend, Alison.'

David looked at Mrs Charles sharply. 'Carol Roper? Where does she fit in all of this?'

Mrs Charles smiled grimly. 'Jack Graves, it would appear, had quite a busy itinerary on Saturday afternoon.'

'Don't talk in riddles to me, Madame!' snapped Merton. 'Are you saying Graves met this girl as well on Saturday afternoon . . . this Carol Roper?'

She nodded. 'Carol Roper is expecting Jack Graves's child; is understandably quite desperate about the situation. And now that I know, or I think I know, the whole story of what really happened on Saturday afternoon, one can perhaps see why he reacted as he did to the discovery of Alison's body in the boot of his car. He was already implicated in a roundabout way in Judith Caldicott's murder through his having been at or near the scene of the crime when it was committed, and as one by one, his other marital infidelities came to light, he knew that one way or another everything was going to conspire against him and make him guilty in everyone's eyes. Worse, his wife — a rather cold, shrewish woman, I've always suspected (the harsh, unforgiving sort), would turn on him in any event, and make his life an absolute hell. And so he took the quick and easy way out for them all. For himself, for his wife, and for his father. He shot himself. But not because he was a murderer and he thought his sins had found him out, but because he was a philanderer who knew his wife would make him pay dearly for it for the rest of his life.'

'How do you know all this?' asked Merton. 'About Graves and the Roper girl?'

'Alison Cockburn's brother, Richard, told me — Yesterday afternoon after Alison's funeral,' she explained to David. She turned back to Merton. In her hand was Alison's note to her. 'It all came out while I was questioning Richard about an anonymous note which Alison slipped inside the newspaper that was delivered to me on Saturday morning — the day she was killed. This was why Alison was killed, Mr Merton. Because she wrote to somebody (me), and her killer, who knew there was a letter of some sort and that Alison had her suspicions about him and was dreadfully upset by the things she was thinking, realised that he had failed (I believe) to allay her fears and doubts about him, and that she would eventually — if she hadn't already done it in the letter Richard had told him about — betray him. I have good reason for thinking that Alison's killer probably searched her room thoroughly for the letter — which Richard had told him he had seen Alison conceal in one of the drawers in her dressing-table — and when he couldn't find it anywhere, he knew he had to act. He had to kill her before she had a chance to talk to someone about the things that were troubling her . . . Like whether or not it was true that some years ago, certain vital components on the motor bike one of Judith Caldicott's teenaged boy-friends was riding when he was killed, had been deliberately tampered with, as Judith claimed at the time. I think Alison hoped that I'd take her fears to Judith's uncle, a policeman — Michael Caldicott — and that he'd dismiss the allegation once and for all as being absolute nonsense.'

Merton had taken the note from her and read it. He looked up at her; waited.

She went on, 'Do you remember what Cyril said to me at his house the other morning when he and I were discussing a boy named Barry Edmonds and his motor bike accident and the members of St Anthony's choir?'

Merton scratched his scalp. 'Vaguely.'

'As I've said, Mr Merton: Cyril deals in specifics. I should've known that the boy played some major part in Barry Edmond's motor bike accident, and therefore in Judith Caldicott's murder. I'm talking now about the boy who sang like a bullfrog and whom Cyril relegated to the back of the choir. A boy who in the normal course of events, and if it hadn't been for a girl he liked to fantasise about sexually, wouldn't have wanted to sing in any choir! An immature boy who was then and is now, sexually perverted, inadequate, and who I think, even in those days, probably spied on Judith late at night from the common ground beyond her bedroom window as she undressed for bed. A boy another girl — Judith's best friend — fancied, and over whom, I also have good reason for thinking, the two girls ultimately fell out with one another (not because Judith liked the boy or encouraged him in any way, but because her friend was jealous of her and of this boy's obsessive infatuation with her). A boy who couldn't sing in tune, but who nevertheless had one very specialised skill, even at that young age. A natural skill which, when he became insanely jealous of Judith's friendship with an older, and therefore undoubtedly much more sophisticated boy, he then put to good use, and with quite deliberate malice aforethought, eliminated the competition forever.' The clairvoyant looked at David. 'A boy dominated by his mother— The threatening feminine influence which *The Moon* card in Judith's Tarot readings, forewarned lurked constantly in the background.'

Mrs Charles hesitated; seemed momentarily distracted by something; vaguely worried. Then, looking steadily at David, she added, 'A very strong, very determined woman and one we would all be well-advised not to underestimate.'

The look on Mrs Charles's face made David feel uneasy. He didn't understand her, he never would, but he had to admit that she had a very special gift. He would hesitate to call it second sight, he didn't believe in such things, but at that moment, he knew instinctively that she was suddenly concerned for him personally, warning him to be careful.

'Go on, Madame,' said Merton in a quiet voice when she paused. 'I'm listening.'

She continued to look at David for a moment or two, then seemed to give herself a little shake; looked back at Merton and said, 'I wanted Cyril to be here tonight while I talked to you so that he could confirm the identity of this boy. It would never have occurred to me that he was an ex-member of St Anthony's choir. I didn't realise that he came from Gidding; that all three of them attended the same high school, and that this was where they all originally met one another many years ago when they were in their early teens. I had no idea that he too knew Judith and had known her so well.'

Merton sighed. 'I think I'm beginning to get your drift.' He dragged a hand wearily down his face. 'I hope, at the end of all this, you're not going to turn round and tell me that other than for this one solid piece of evidence regarding their all having known one another as teenagers, you can prove to me that the young man had the opportunity to carry out these murders as well as a motive.'

'There was no motive for Judith Caldicott's murder, Mr Merton. That's if, by motive, you mean he deliberately set out to kill her the way he killed Alison.' Mrs Charles shook her head. 'Judith's murder was, in a sense, a *crime passionnel*, sexually motivated. He wanted Judith sexually, was incapable of having her because of this serious flaw in his make-up; she mocked him, scorned his manhood, and he lost his head. And if I'm right about this, a good defence lawyer, I'm sure you'll agree, would've got him a considerably reduced sentence for his crime. Unfortunately, he didn't stop there. He panicked . . . Ran to the one person who I think knew of his sexual inadequacies and, as so often happens in cases of this nature, protects the individual concerned.'

'In this instance,' said Merton with a sigh, 'not a wife, but the boy's mother.'

Mrs Charles nodded. 'But to answer your question . . . No,

Mr Merton: the only proof I can offer is that which my brother can provide. That this boy was once in his choir and sang badly out of tune. As for the rest of it —' she shook her head; looked doubtful. 'If the young man and his mother refuse to waver and stand fast over their stories, then short of someone actually having seen Alison climb into the Jacksons' car with him while he was giving it a road test, I don't see how you are going to shake them into confessing their complicity. I don't doubt that every detail of the account which Carol Roper has given me of her meeting with Mr Graves that afternoon is completely accurate. It is nevertheless full of holes which a clever lawyer will be only too quick to spot.'

She paused; shook her head regretfully. 'I know that it was Dennis Pendlebury who killed Judith Caldicott; that he was the husky-voiced man who rang to cancel her appointment with me; that the reason his voice was husky was not necessarily an attempt on his part to conceal his true identity from me, but probably simply because he was getting over the Gidding flu (as are so many of us living here in the village), and which, according to Alison's brother, Richard, he (Dennis) introduced into the Cockburn household. I also know that Dennis Pendlebury killed his fiancée because she guessed — or rather, remembering his obsessive teenage crush on her best friend, feared — he was Judith's killer, and he was afraid that she would betray him. But then again, it could also have been Jack Graves who killed both girls. The fact that, according to Carol Roper, he was in his own car and not the Jacksons' when he picked her up on Saturday afternoon will prove very little. Carol is too vague about times; and a good lawyer will have little difficulty in convincing a jury that it was still possible for Graves to have met and talked to her, then returned to the garage, changed cars, picked up Alison a little later on while test driving the Jacksons' car and then killed her.'

David interrupted. 'Excuse me . . . But aren't you two forgetting something? My aunt. She's going to be absolutely fizzing about all of this when she finds out that somebody's actually got away with pulling the wool over her eyes. She'll have to take it out on somebody; and I'm the one she's going to blame for it!' He narrowed his eyes thoughtfully. 'Why not defuse the poor old girl and let her have a chance to save her face by giving her something useful to do for a change?'

Mrs Charles and Merton looked at him.

'What would you suggest?' asked Merton.

He smiled. 'Let's talk about it, shall we?'

CHAPTER TWENTY-TWO

'Making a spectacle of herself at the girl's funeral,' muttered the old lady as Mrs Pendlebury helped her into her cardigan. 'She ought to be ashamed of herself.'

'Who's that you're talking about now, Miss Sayer?' inquired the other woman, assisting Miss Sayer into the pink, painted wicker chair by her bedroom window and then kneeling to put on the old lady's shoes for her. Miss Sayer was gradually becoming more mobile and was able to move about with the aid of a walking-stick so long as she exercised great care and made no attempt to hurry.

'Roper's eldest, of course,' replied Miss Sayer. 'Alison Cockburn's bridesmaid.'

'Oh, you mean Carol,' said Mrs Pendlebury. 'How do you know she made a spectacle of herself at the funeral? You weren't there.'

'I've got ears!' The old lady suddenly twisted round and glared through the window. 'There's that fool Forbes! I suppose he's off down to Roper's field to sit and keep the cows company again. You'd think he'd have the decency to keep himself out of the public spotlight for a few weeks.'

'Good heavens, Miss Sayer!' exclaimed Mrs Pendlebury. 'Whatever for? The man's completely innocent, an unfortunate victim of circumstances, that's all.'

'That's as may be,' said the old lady with one of her dark looks. 'You mark my words; we haven't heard the last of this. Not by a long chalk. *Pah!* Jack Graves never killed those girls. Only a fool would think that. A mouse, that's what he was; been one ever since he was in short pants. His kind are all the same. They sneak out of their hole and play about while they think they're safe and nobody's watching them, but the moment they scent trouble, they go scuttling back home to mother and hide behind her skirts quaking in their boots till it's safe for them to come out again.'

'From what I've read in the newspapers, the police wouldn't appear to have the slightest doubt that Mr Graves was the man they were looking for,' commented Mrs Pendlebury.'

'What would they know?' snorted the old lady. 'That's what they said when they arrested that fool Forbes. And look where he is now? Charging down the road, large as life, without a care in the world!' She snorted again. 'Graves was a coward. He should've brazened it out, like that fool Forbes did. The truth will out in the finish. You just wait and see if I'm not right.'

Mrs Pendlebury finished tying the laces on Miss Sayer's shoes, then got up. 'You talk almost as if you know something the police don't,' she remarked.

'I've got eyes in my head,' said the old lady, still looking out of the window. She leaned forward suddenly. 'Binoculars . . . *Quick!*' she demanded.

The glasses were on the dressing-table and Mrs Pendlebury pushed them towards her.

'Now what?' muttered the old lady as she peered through them.

Mrs Pendlebury went and stood at the window looking down at the road beyond. Carol Roper was walking hurriedly in the direction of Mrs Charles's bungalow.

'You mark my words . . .' muttered the old lady, her eyes glued to the glasses.

'Yes, Miss Sayer?' inquired Mrs Pendlebury when no more was said.

Miss Sayer looked round at her as though surprised that she was still there. Then, resuming her surveillance of the road and the people walking along it, she said, 'That girl knows something . . . If I know anything about people, she's on her way to talk to that woman up the road.' She snorted softly; put the binoculars aside. 'Well, she's in for a big disappointment. Mrs High and Mighty Charles caught the Gidding bus first thing this morning: won't be back until late this afternoon, as like as not.'

'Carol Roper?' Mrs Pendlebury was astonished. 'What on earth do you mean when you say she knows something?'

Miss Sayer looked at the other woman scornfully. 'You don't imagine that Beryl Fisher was the only stupid little fool that Graves was stringing along, do you? That man's father was exactly the same; secretly engaged to be married to four different girls, all at the same time, and not one of them knew a thing about the other and yet they all lived and worked cheek by jowl here in the village!' She snorted. 'I could tell you some stories about that Sam Graves!'

The old lady suddenly leaned forward again, narrowing her eyes into a fixed squint as she gazed into the distance. 'She's hanging about out on the porch . . . Going to wait, by the looks of things. She'll need the patience of Job if I'm right and Mrs Charles has gone out for the day.'

Mrs Pendlebury stepped nearer to the window and looked along the road at the clairvoyant's bungalow.

'What could she want to talk to Mrs Charles about, I wonder?' said Mrs Pendlebury in a musing voice.

'It'll have something to do with Jack Graves, you mark my words,' said Miss Sayer. 'I know the signs . . . All that blubbering in the church; showing herself up like that. I don't know what the world's coming to!'

'Most of us were upset and weeping, Miss Sayer,' said Mrs Pendlebury, turning to make the bed. 'It was a most distressing occasion.'

'*Pah!*' said the old lady. 'The girl's got a guilty conscience. Plain as the nose on your face! She knows something.'

'You keep saying that, Miss Sayer,' said Mrs Pendlebury, plumping up the pillows, 'but what on earth could she possibly know?'

Miss Sayer didn't answer. For the moment, Carol Roper had her undivided attention, and the old lady watched her closely.

At length, Miss Sayer said, 'Maybe Alison told her something. Or Jack Graves . . . Graves, I'd say. He's the more likely of the two. You mark my words, Graves has been frolicking in the fields with her, too.'

'That's a dreadful slur, Miss Sayer.' Mrs Pendlebury looked dismayed; shocked. 'You should be ashamed of yourself for even thinking such a thing!'

Miss Sayer gave her one of her dark, hooded looks; made no comment. Mrs Pendlebury went on straightening the bed. 'Would you like me to bring your cup of tea up here, or would you prefer to have it when you come downstairs?' she asked after a moment.

Miss Sayer didn't reply. '*Aha* . . .' she said. 'Just as I thought! She's off up the road to that fool Forbes's place. She's going to ask him where she can find Mrs Charles.'

'No, she can't be,' said Mrs Pendlebury, crossing to the window to see for herself. 'She must be going somewhere else. She would've passed Mr Forbes on the road a few minutes ago and know he's not in.'

'He'd ducked through that gap in the hedgerow not far from Roper's wall and disappeared long before she came round the corner.' Miss Sayer paused. Then she said, 'That one's got something she wants to get off her chest, all right.' The old lady screwed her head round to look at the clock on the mantel-shelf. 'What time is it? I'm not having anyone accuse me of falling asleep on the job again and turning all the clocks backwards and forwards to cover up my tracks. Nobody pulls the wool over my eyes and gets away with it.'

Mrs Pendlebury looked at her in surprise. 'Whatever are you talking about, Miss Sayer?'

'That girl up the road . . . If anything happens to her this morning, it's not going to be my fault. They needn't bother to come to me with any more of their lame excuses and think I'll —'

Mrs Pendlebury interrupted her impatiently. 'No, what you said about falling asleep on the job . . . What did you mean by that?'

'Oh, that,' said Miss Sayer. She picked up the binoculars again and looked through them; made no further comment.

Mrs Pendlebury watched her for a moment. Then, crossing to the door, she said, 'I'll go and make the tea now. I'll come back up and help you down the stairs when it's ready. Are you warm enough? Would you like me to turn on the gas fire for you?'

Miss Sayer's eyes were glued to the back of the girl walking along the road in the direction of Cyril Forbes's property. She heard what was said to her, but made no reply.

Mrs Pendlebury hesitated, looked across the room at the old lady, then closed the door behind her and went downstairs. She paused in the hall; glanced back up the stairs, then went quickly into the living-room; closed the door quietly. She made a telephone call first, then she opened Miss Sayer's sewing-basket and removed a reel of strong, clear nylon thread. Next, she went out to the kitchen, emptied the contents of the tea-caddy into the sink and then sluiced out the sink with water until all the tea-leaves were flushed away and the sink was left spotlessly clean. Finally, she went back upstairs.

Ten minutes later, she stood at the foot of the stairs and called up to Miss Sayer. Mrs Pendlebury was wearing her hat and coat and wrapped round her throat was the warm woollen scarf which she had been knitting in between taking care of Miss Sayer, and which she had finished shortly before going up to bed the previous night.

'I'm just popping out for some tea, Miss Sayer.' Mrs Pendlebury paused. There was no response. 'I'll only be a few minutes. Now, don't you do anything silly while I'm gone, will you? You make sure you stay right where you are until I get back. It's still too soon for you to be tackling these stairs on your own.'

'*Silly cat!*' muttered Miss Sayer under her breath in response. Stan North was the current object of her attention. He was picking something carefully off the leaves of a clump of blackberry growing in the hedgerow. He looked up as Mrs Pendlebury came out of Miss Sayer's front door and watched her hurry away in the direction of the Post Office Stores. Miss Sayer was watching her, too; and as soon as she was out of sight, she reached for her walking-stick, and then, with her other hand, pushed herself up awkwardly onto her feet. It was a moment or two before she felt completely steady and sure of herself. Then, leaning heavily on her stick, she stepped out carefully towards the door.

Carol Roper looked hesitantly at Cyril Forbes's front door. She was thinking about Judith Caldicott, about what had happened to her — in that room there, Carol supposed, frowning a little at the net-curtained bay-window to the right of the door. She presumed that was the living-room, where it had happened. She could hear a cat mewing somewhere inside the house, and a second later, the net curtains on the living-room window were pushed aside and Cyril's fearsomely antisocial black cat, James, prowled up and down the window-ledge. He had lost an ear in a skirmish since Carol last saw him which made him look even less friendly and sociable.

She watched the cat for a few moments, then went to the side of the house and peeked round it at the oast-house. There was no way, she thought, that she was going anywhere near that place, that was for sure! It gave her the creeps.

She looked round with a start as a small pick-up van drew up, then walked diffidently towards it as Dennis Pendlebury got out and came over to her.

'Hello, Dennis,' she said. 'I don't think Mr Forbes is in right now.' She looked back over her shoulder at the house. 'He's not answering the door. I've rung the bell twice.'

Dennis was surprised. 'He was there five minutes ago. He phoned me to come out and fetch his bike in for repairs. Have you tried the door?'

As he spoke he went up to the door and turned the knob. The door opened readily, with just the softest of clicks. Dennis glanced back over his shoulder at Carol, who looked scared. 'Come on; it's all right. He's probably out the back in the kitchen.'

He strode ahead of her down the hall and disappeared

through a door at the end of it. Carol hesitated, then followed him into the morning-room.

'Damn!' said Dennis, looking round at her. 'The stupid old goat must've gone wandering off somewhere: he's not here, either. Well, I haven't got all day to hang about waiting for him. He can fetch the bike in himself.' He looked at her curiously. 'What did you want with him, anyway?'

'Well, actually, it wasn't Mr Forbes I wanted to see. I'm looking for Mrs Charles.' Carol hesitated. 'It's funny us running into one another like this. I've been worrying myself sick about something and maybe you can help me. I know this is an awful thing to do — I mean, I shouldn't really be discussing this with you so soon after your upset over losing Alison and everything, but I'm so worried . . . I couldn't sleep at all last night for thinking about it. It's about Mr Graves . . . I don't think he was the one who — well, you know.' She paused; looked down at the floor. 'He didn't do it, Dennis; he couldn't have. He was with me. I'm so scared . . . I should tell somebody about this, I know; but what are my mum and dad going to say when they find out that I've been seeing Mr Graves behind everybody's back? What do you think I should do? It's wrong not to tell, isn't it?' She looked up at him. Her face was pale and anxious. 'Everyone's saying that Mr Graves picked Alison up in one of his customer's cars. But they're wrong, Dennis; he couldn't have done what they're saying. Somebody's got everything all mixed up.'

'Why couldn't Graves have been in the Jacksons' car like the police said?' he asked.

'Because he was in his own car, that's why. We sat in it together and talked for ages.' She looked at Dennis plaintively. 'You can see why I'm so upset. How could he possibly be with me and with Alison at the same time, and in two different cars?'

'You've got your times muddled,' he said.

She shook her head slowly. 'No, I don't think so, Dennis. I know exactly what time it was, to the minute. And I can prove it . . . Well, not me, exactly. I wouldn't know how to go about these things. But Mrs Charles will know. That's why I want to see her. She'll go to Mr Sayer — Miss Sayer's nephew (he was a policeman once, wasn't he?) — and he'll tell her what I should do. It's wrong that Mr Graves should be made to take the blame for something that I know he couldn't have done. I've got to tell someone or I'll go mad.'

'Well, I still think the police have got the right man, myself, but I'll give you a lift, if you like. Mrs Charles might be shopping down in the village. You'll probably find her talking to Mrs Cockburn in the Post Office Stores.'

'Okay,' said Carol. 'Thanks.'

He stepped aside and she preceded him into the hall; walked quickly on ahead. As she reached the hall-stand, she sensed rather than actually saw or felt Dennis move up a little too closely behind her, and she gave a sudden start forward and then turned quickly round to face him. In his right hand, he was holding the large monkey-wrench he had taken from one of the deep pockets of his greasy mechanic's overalls.

They stared at one another.

'It *was* you!' she gasped at length. 'I thought so. *You* killed Alison!'

Dennis seemed to collapse under the weight of her accusation; looked desperately frightened; close to tears. 'I'm sorry, I'm sorry! Honestly, Carol: I didn't want to hurt her, but I had to, I had to! Mother said it was the only way. She made me.'

Carol backed from him. Her face registered her disgust. 'I never liked you. You're sick. You should be put away!'

'Mother said they won't . . . Not if I kill you, too. She promised me.'

She sneered at him. 'My mother always said your mother was too good to be true. She's even madder than you are! Sick in the head. Twisted!'

'Don't say that, Carol,' he pleaded, advancing on her. 'You mustn't talk like that about her. You must believe me, my mother would do anything for me.'

'Yes, lad!' snapped a stern voice behind him. 'I don't doubt it!'

Carol looked past Dennis at Chief Superintendent Merton, who had stepped out into the hall from the room which Cyril

Forbes used as a study, then she paled to a deathly shade of white, covered her mouth with her hand, turned, and then rushed outside and was violently sick.

Stan North was standing at Miss Sayer's front gate when Mrs Pendlebury returned from her shopping trip into the village. He looked worried.

'Thank goodness you're back,' he greeted her, without preamble. 'I was just trying to make up my mind what I should do. I think something terrible's happened to Miss Sayer. I was working over there in the hedgerow —' he pointed across the road '— and there was this dreadful, blood-curdling scream. Fair made my hair stand on end!' He hesitated; seemed suddenly doubtful. 'It sounded like a scream. You know me . . . I get engrossed in what I'm doing and somebody could let off a fire-cracker right beside me and I'd never notice. It might've been a bird. A magpie attacking one of the smaller birds, a sparrow. They can be right vicious beasts when the mood's upon 'em, and kick up a devil of a racket.'

Mrs Pendlebury looked anxiously at the cottage. 'I'd better go straight in and make sure everything's all right. I do hope the old lady hasn't tackled those stairs on her own. I told her I'd be back in a few minutes, but you know what she's like. She will insist on doing things her way; won't listen to anybody! I only popped out for some tea . . .'

As she finished speaking, Mrs Pendlebury quickly unlatched the gate and then hurried up the path, unlocked the front door and disappeared through it.

Stan North watched from the gate. Then he turned and went back across the road and continued with his work in the hedgerow.

Mrs Pendlebury closed the door and stood with her back to it; let out a sigh of relief. Miss Sayer was lying in an ominously silent, crumpled heap, face-down on the floor, at the foot of the staircase. Her walking-stick was lying on the stairs where it had been dropped.

Quickly, Mrs Pendlebury stepped over Miss Sayer's body and hurried up the stairs, took a sharply-pointed pair of scissors from out of her handbag, swiftly cut the long strands of nylon thread which she had stretched taut across the head of the stairs prior to her going down to the village, then hastily gathered up the thread and stuffed it, together with the scissors, into her handbag. She wasn't sure what Stan North had done after she had left him standing at the gate, and more or less expected that at any moment, he would knock on the door to inquire if everything was all right. And everything *was* all right. That — removing the nylon thread — was the last little detail taken care of. All she had to do now was to telephone for an ambulance and report that there had been a nasty accident: that, unfortunately, while her back had been turned for those few short minutes when she was out shopping in the village for some tea, poor (pigheaded!) Miss Sayer had ignored the warning that she had been given and had attempted to walk down the stairs on her own. And, of course, everyone knew what a wilfully determined old woman Margaret Sayer was; that you could warn her about something until you were blue in the face and that she would take not a blind bit of notice of you and do exactly as she pleased!

Mrs Pendlebury turned quickly and looked down the stairs as the living-room door suddenly opened and David Sayer came out into the hall holding his aunt's binoculars in his right hand. He looked down at his aunt. 'Come along, Auntie. You're missing all the excitement. You'll never believe what's going on at the other end of the road.'

It was a moment or two before the woman standing at the head of the stairs was able to grasp the full implications of the strange little scene she was witnessing. And then, as David helped his aunt up onto her feet and made her comfortable on the bottom step while he went to fetch her stick from off the stairs, Mrs Pendlebury snatched the scissors from out of her handbag, and with a savage, almost primeval roar, she rushed down at him as he climbed towards her.

CHAPTER TWENTY-THREE

'I still can't quite see what part that cup of tea of Aunt Margaret's played, what was so important about it,' confessed Jean Sayer later that same day when she and David slipped away from his aunt for a few minutes to call on Mrs Charles and discuss the successful outcome of the stratagem which David had devised (and which had involved the co-operation of his aunt, Carol Roper and Stan North) for forcing the Pendleburys to give themselves away.

Dennis Pendlebury had been taken into custody and he and his mother had been driven to the Gidding Constabulary for further questioning in connection with the murder of Judith Caldicott and the death of Alison Cockburn. Cyril Forbes had returned quietly to his home, Mrs Charles to hers. Carol Roper — who confessed to Mrs Charles afterwards that she had never been so scared in all her life (she was sure Dennis knew all along that she was terrified of him), and who swore that she would never do anything like that again for anybody! — had gone home to discuss her future with her parents. Miss Sayer was talking on the telephone to her friend, Venie Jackson, bringing her up to date with all the latest developments and the principal role she had played in them, when her nephew and Jean had sneaked off; would probably be there for hours, according to David.

Mrs Charles smiled at Jean in response to her having admitted to being confused over the exact importance of Miss Sayer's afternoon tea on the day that Judith Caldicott was murdered. 'But for you,' said Mrs Charles, 'and the remarks you made about Miss Sayer after you'd visited her the other day, we might never have seen anything at all unusual about it. It suddenly came back to me after Carol Roper refused a second cup of tea when she visited me the night before last . . . That Miss Sayer is in the habit of becoming quite irritable if anyone forgets and offers her another cup of tea. And yet the day my brother walked past her cottage while she was having her afternoon tea, she broke with that apparently hard and fast rule and asked for a refill because she was thirsty. Certainly, it was an unusually warm day for September, but nothing like warm enough, I shouldn't have thought, to give a person an abnormally dry throat. This, I felt, raised an interesting possibility which until then, had never occurred to me; that Miss Sayer hadn't taken anything at all to drink that afternoon, and that the empty cup she could see by her side, had been deliberately emptied by someone — and this could only have happened if she'd dozed off for a time — to make her think she'd drunk her tea. I immediately got Cyril to come straight over — this was while Carol was still here with me — and I asked him whether Miss Sayer could've been cat-napping when he saw her sitting in her living-room window. He admitted that it was a possibility. He only glanced at her as he went past. She was sitting in the window, as usual, and he assumed the rest. That she had seen him.'

'Your aunt's eyes are inclined to be rather hooded,' Jean said to her husband. 'Sometimes I'm not sure if they're open and she's looking at me. And I'm talking about when I'm sitting right up close to her!' Jean looked back at Mrs Charles. 'Mrs Pendlebury saw your brother walking past Aunt Margaret's cottage, and she knew Aunt Margaret was asleep at the time, so she simply emptied her cup to trick her into thinking that she'd been awake the whole time and quietly drinking her tea, and that because she'd had her tea, drunk it all up at the usual time, she'd stick to her story about not having seen Mr Forbes at all that afternoon —' Jean broke off with a frown. 'I can see all that. But how did Mrs Pendlebury know that it was going to be so important to her personally that David's aunt should discredit Mr Forbes's account of his movements that afternoon if the police came to her for help with their inquiries into Judith Caldicott's murder?'

'My brother wasn't the only person Miss Sayer missed

seeing that afternoon while she was dozing,' said Mrs Charles. 'She missed the drama that was taking place right under her nose, in her own kitchen. Dennis Pendlebury panicked after he'd killed Judith. He hadn't meant to kill her. Judith turned on him over the trick he'd played on her in luring her to my brother's house, and she reviled him; told him that he was sick in the head, that he'd always been sick in the head, a sexually perverted misfit, even when they were teenagers; and from there things got tragically out of hand and before he knew what he was doing, he'd choked her to death. For all anybody knows, simply to cut off the sound of her voice and put an end to the horrible things she was saying to him.

'He told his mother that he remembers putting his hands round Judith's throat and nothing else. He had some kind of blackout. Then when he came out of this trance — or whatever it was that came over him when Judith turned on him the way she did — and he realised what he'd done, he cut across the fields on foot to Miss Sayer's cottage, went round to the back door, his mother let him in, and he broke down in tears and confessed everything to her. She calmed him, gave him one of Miss Sayer's sharp kitchen knives (which he returned to his mother later and she replaced in the knife-rack), and then she told him exactly what he must do. He would have to go back to my brother's house as quickly as he could and partly undress the girl, cut her vocal chords so that suspicion would fall on my brother, and then tie round her throat the black lace brassiere he (Dennis) had stolen from off Mrs Caldicott's washing-line on one of the occasions when he was spying on Judith from the stretch of common ground at the bottom of her parents' garden (something he'd done frequently since Judith's return home to Gidding) to make it appear that it was a sex crime. Mrs Pendlebury was latterly the matron of a geriatric nursing home, but as a young woman, she'd worked as a theatre sister.'

Jean shuddered. 'She knew where, how to cut the girl's throat.'

Mrs Charles nodded, and Jean said, with another shudder, 'Horrible.'

Mrs Charles went on, 'Dennis did exactly as Mother said, after which he simply returned to the garage and got on with his work. In the meanwhile, Mrs Pendlebury emptied Miss Sayer's cup and altered the clock in the living-room to reinforce Miss Sayer's belief that she had drunk her tea, and that the time of day — this was when Mrs Pendlebury unobtrusively woke her up — was a few minutes after three o'clock when it was actually nearer to three-thirty. They then carried on as if everything was perfectly normal, with Mrs Pendlebury, of course, casually readjusting the clock to the correct time during the remainder of the afternoon. As for Dennis, it never occurred to Mr Graves to question the young man's whereabouts that afternoon while he was with Beryl Fisher in Whitethatch Cottage. Dennis was his alibi, wasn't he? Not the other way round! Dennis was expected to tell everyone — Mrs Graves specifically, should she have inquired, which she didn't . . . not on that occasion — that Mr Graves was in the garage with him all afternoon. This was where Mr Graves expected the young man to be, providing him with a cover, whereas in actual fact, it was Mr Graves who was unwittingly covering for Dennis.'

'I can understand a mother wanting to protect her son, but what a despicable thing to do, pinning — or rather, *trying* to pin — the blame on Mr Forbes,' said Jean.

'She loves the boy, he's all she's got,' said Mrs Charles with a sad smile. 'Some women will fight tooth and claw to protect their menfolk, no matter how dreadful their crimes. And women like Mrs Pendlebury can always convince themselves that it was the girl's fault, that the girl deliberately led the young man on and drove him to commit his crime.'

Mrs Charles paused; looked reflective. 'It bothered me all along that there might've been more luck involved in the way Judith Caldicott's murderer had got away with his crime, than actual careful planning on his part; and with hindsight, I think this was definitely the case. Everything fell into place for Dennis. Nobody saw my brother; and nobody saw Dennis (other than his mother, of course). Mr Graves would swear (were he asked) — and for his own personal reasons, having been guilty of committing a lesser crime of his own that afternoon which had to be covered up! — that Dennis was in the garage all afternoon working on a customer's car. And my brother was the perfect suspect, the man most likely to have committed the murder. Which Mrs Pendlebury was only too quick to see. The Pendleburys lived in Gidding prior to moving in with Mrs Pendlebury's widowed sister here in the village, and Dennis, Judith and Alison Cockburn all attended the same high school — and for a time, when Dennis's fantasising about Judith was at its zenith, he even sang in St Anthony's choir alongside her, I discovered later from Cyril. Mother and son were well aware that it was my brother who had originally recognised Judith's singing talent and encouraged her to develop it. And they knew it would be reasonable to expect people to assume that he'd been severely disappointed, after having arranged for her to take up formal voice training, that she'd given it all up for the pop scene, and that this then was his motive for slashing her vocal chords. It was his way, people would think, of punishing her for the abuse of her voice.'

'Nobody knew that the Pendleburys came from Gidding originally?' asked Jean.

'The Cockburns knew,' replied Mrs Charles. 'As I've said, Dennis went to school in Gidding with Alison and Judith. Alison had a crush on him ever since she first set eyes on him. Tilly — her mother — said Alison decided that she was going to marry him years ago, while they were still at school. Dennis, it seems, was never quite so keen on her. Nor was Mrs Pendlebury; or so she confided to Miss Sayer. (And Alison never liked Mrs Pendlebury, who was apparently openly critical of her to Dennis; always finding fault with her.) I spoke to Tilly a little while ago, and she told me that on reflection, it was always very much a one-sided relationship. She couldn't remember ever once having seen any normal outward display of affection between the two of them, though there's no doubt in her mind that Alison was deeply in love with him. Quite frankly, I doubt that he was capable of displaying any kind of natural affection for a member of the opposite sex.'

'Poor girl,' murmured Jean.

'Yes,' agreed Mrs Charles.

'I'm surprised that she turned him in,' remarked Jean.

'She didn't. Not really,' said Mrs Charles. 'I think she must've realised that if she was right — and I've no doubt that she prayed to the bitter end that she was wrong about him, and he hadn't killed Judith — then he had some very serious sexual problems; there could be no wedding, no rosy future for them ever. She obviously knew that Dennis, as a teenager had had these abnormal sexual fantasies about Judith, and that he used to hang about at the bottom of her garden late at night watching her undress for bed. (I'm inclined to think Alison was so jealous of Judith over this that it was the direct cause of the break-up of their close friendship.) And Alison knew, or had heard the rumour, that Dennis had fixed up Judith's boy-friend's motor bike for him as a favour (Dennis was only a gifted amateur then; he didn't start working for Jack Graves until after he and his mother had moved over here to the village to live), and that he'd deliberately tampered with certain vital parts of the machine so that the boy would have an accident. Knowing all these things about Dennis, it would take a very brave — and exceedingly foolish — young woman to think that she could go ahead and marry such a man and not live to count the cost.'

'He saw Judith again . . . where?' asked Jean. 'Here, or in Gidding?'

'Here, I would say, to begin with,' replied Mrs Charles. 'He saw her whizzing past the garage every Wednesday afternoon in that sexy (to him, that is) little sports car of hers, and his obsession with her, the fantasising, started all over again. Everyone knew what she was doing in the village, that she was consulting me regularly for a reading of the Tarot; and Dennis simply used his knowledge of us all — of Cyril, what he usually did of a Wednesday, what I used to do each Wednesday afternoon before Judith came back home to Gidding and started consulting me — and made the most of it . . . Wove all of it into what had become a deadly fantasy. And with remarkable success to begin with. Nothing went wrong for him. He didn't even have to try and make things go right. Everything simply fell into place. My brother became steadily more deeply enmeshed, and Dennis that much safer. Until Alison started to get worried. So worried that she couldn't stop crying. People naturally thought it was pre-wedding jitters, nerves. And it was, up to a point, but not in the way that everyone was thinking. Everyone except Dennis, of course. He knew that she suspected him. Perhaps he even tried to allay her fears. He knew he'd failed when Richard — Alison's eleven-year-old brother — told him that he'd seen Alison writing a letter to her secret lover, Mr Graves. Dennis knew this was nonsense, that Alison couldn't stand the sight of Jack Graves, and he guessed, from Richard's graphic description of Alison's secretiveness over the letter, that its contents more than likely concerned him and his obsession with Judith Caldicott. So the first opportunity he got (he's been taking his meals with the Cockburns while his mother's been looking after Miss Sayer), he slipped up to Alison's room and went through it looking for the letter. (Richard, incidentally, got blamed for the mess Dennis left behind him.) Then when he couldn't find any trace of it, he turned once more to his mother, and again she came to the rescue and told him exactly what he must do.

'And that,' continued Mrs Charles with a grim smile, 'was where their incredibly good luck suddenly started to run out on them. They made their first mistake. So far as I was concerned, anyway. Instead of chancing to luck, the way they had before, and which had always worked so remarkably well for them, they sat down and planned their crime. Used the same ploy that Dennis had used to lure Judith to my brother's house. He rang Mrs Blackmore pretending to be Mr Cockburn — Dennis's voice was a little husky from the very bad bout of Gidding flu he was still trying to shake off, although quite obviously, nowhere near as husky as when he spoke to me several days earlier pretending to be Judith's father or I would've recognised it when I phoned him at the garage early that evening after he'd spoken to Mrs Blackmore on the phone and cancelled Alison's appointment with her.'

Mrs Charles shook her head slowly. 'I couldn't understand that. It wasn't necessary. Why cancel her appointment (which Alison's abductor obviously knew all about) when all he had to do was to waylay her *en route* to her appointment and spirit her off? He should have left well enough alone: left us all to draw our own conclusions about her disappearance; that she'd simply wanted to get away and be on her own for a time, away from all the pressures of preparing for her wedding. It made me think very seriously about the person who had abducted her, and for the first time I saw the possibility that he wasn't the clever, cunning criminal that I'd thought. He was simply lucky; and by the law of averages, in time that luck was going to run out for him. And, of course, it had. Dennis and his mother thought (as did Jack Graves) that again, one would cover for the other. It was a stupid mistake to make to try and link the two crimes. Dennis, in particular, was nowhere near clever enough for that. He and his mother should've left Cyril to take the blame for Judith's murder, and chanced to luck again that they could so arrange things for Jack Graves to take the blame for Alison's death.'

Mrs Charles paused; smiled faintly. 'He was, after all, tailor-made for the part. Perfect. Jack Graves had been pestering Alison (Richard Cockburn could testify to that), and Dennis knew that Jack Graves was a committed philanderer, that lately he'd been seeing someone every Wednesday afternoon. Dennis also knew, because of the special arrangement Mr Graves had made over the Jacksons' car — that he'd return it to them personally in Gidding — that in all probability, Mr Graves was making the most of his opportunity and meeting his Wednesday girl-friend again while he was out. What Dennis didn't know was that there were *two* girl-friends, one of whom phoned Mr Graves shortly before Alison finished up work for the day and left to keep her appointment at the vicarage. Carol Roper was the girl who, unbeknown to Dennis, phoned Mr Graves that afternoon and threatened to go to his wife and tell her that they'd been seeing one another, and that she was pregnant, if Mr Graves didn't meet her immediately and talk things over with her.

'Mr Graves told Carol it couldn't be straight away, that he would have to wait for Alison to leave first — in case she spotted them together. Then, when he saw Alison go past the garage and he was sure it was safe, he slipped away, calling out to Dennis that he'd be back in a while and that he'd deliver the Jacksons' car to them then. He got into his car, drove down to the old brewery where he picked up Carol, and then they drove off along one of those overgrown tracks round the back of the brewery to have their talk. Dennis had meanwhile hopped into the Jacksons' car, which he had to road test before it was returned to the Jacksons, and driven off along Roper's road, and then down the lane towards the vicarage, picking up Alison in the pouring rain along the way.'

David took up the narrative. 'Merton hasn't been able to establish yet where Pendlebury killed the girl — frightened her to death, actually. (Merton's inclined to think Pendlebury pulled up somewhere along the road, on one of those turn-offs past the vicarage, and that's when the girl died.) Then Pendlebury returned to the garage, removed her body from the car, did the things his mother had told him to do to it — removed her clothing and wrapped her tights round her throat — then stowed it somewhere and simply got on with his work until Graves returned. Then when Graves took off in the Jacksons' car, Pendlebury transferred the girl's body into the boot of Graves's car, never for one moment suspecting that in so doing, he had in effect exonerated the very person whom he and his mother planned to frame for Alison's murder because this was the car Graves had used for his secret liaison with girl-friend No. 2, Carol Roper, and at the very time that it would later be alleged that he'd murdered Alison.'

'Didn't your aunt spot Dennis as he drove past — that it was him and not Mr Graves in the Jacksons' car?' Jean asked him.

'Mrs Pendlebury took care to warn Dennis to put some-thing up in the front seat to obscure Aunt Margaret's view of the driver. And in any event, it was getting dark and raining heavily. There was no way she could've been really positive who was driving the car.'

'Lord,' said Jean in a soft voice. 'It's hard to say who's the madder of the two. The mother or the son!'

'I wouldn't turn my back on either one of them,' said David.

'I think the mother frightens me most of all,' said Mrs Charles. 'As I've often heard it said down in the village, she really was just a little too good to be true.'

'You can say that again,' murmured David, tentatively fingering the long, jagged slash across his chin and down the left side of his throat where Mrs Pendlebury had lunged at him with the scissors when she had realised that she had been tricked into betraying herself and her son. He smiled ruefully at Mrs Charles. 'You did warn me, though.' He studied her curiously. 'You looked at me and saw something while you were talking to Merton about her, didn't you? That was why you paused and warned us not to underestimate her.'

Mrs Charles smiled faintly. 'You were in shadow, and for a moment or two I was concerned for you and feared the worst.'

He grinned; spoke teasingly. 'Only for a moment or two? What changed things?'

'The shadow lightened, and with it the danger which I knew you were ultimately going to have to face at the hands of this woman. There would be a serious confrontation between the two of you, this was inevitable, but you would survive it with your life, if not your entire body —' she smiled '— intact.'

'I'm still cross with you about that,' said Jean, watching him. 'You're too old now to be taking silly risks. That woman had just tried to kill your aunt with the nylon thread she'd stretched across the top of the stairs. She could've just as easily killed you, you know.'

David was inclined to agree with her, although he didn't say so. It was certainly the last thing he had expected to happen, that she would come rushing down the stairs at him the way she had; and the woman had then fought so strongly that he had even thought for a time that she would overpower him before he succeeded in disarming her.

Jean turned to Mrs Charles. 'You must feel very relieved that it's all over. You and your brother have had a terrible time. He's had a very close call.'

Mrs Charles smiled a little. 'Cyril? No, not really. He's very much a survivor. Like Mr Punch. And you know what happened to poor old Jack Ketch when he tried to be too clever with him.'

Jean looked at her husband. 'Jack Ketch? Who's he?'

'Jack Ketch,' David explained, 'is the hangman in the traditional story of *'Punch and Judy'* who unwisely, as it turned out, slipped the noose round Punch's neck for killing Judy and their baby. When they took off the hood covering the head of the man they'd hanged, it was Jack Ketch they found dead. Punch had scarpered.'

Jean looked at Mrs Charles, then back at David. 'Good thing, too,' she said; and they all laughed.